He smiled across at her. 'I promise to be extremely quiet,' he s---

How ... informal ... they were being, Ria thought, now that they were alone together for the first time since he'd kissed her. There was nothing in his expression to suggest that it had crossed his mind since—and how was *she* managing to appear so casual…so completely normal? She'd even stopped herself from blushing—which must be a first.

D0529910

Susanne James has enjoyed creative writing since childhood, completing her first—sadly unpublished—novel by the age of twelve. She has three grown-up children who were, and are, her pride and joy, and who all live happily in Oxfordshire with their families. She was always happy to put the needs of her family before her ambition to write seriously, although along the way some published articles for magazines and newspapers helped to keep the dream alive!

Susanne's big regret is that her beloved husband is no longer here to share the pleasure of her recent success. She now shares her life with Toffee, her young Cavalier King Charles spaniel, who decides when it's time to get up (early) and when a walk in the park is overdue!

Recent titles by the same author:

THE BOSELLI BRIDE
THE PLAYBOY OF PENGARROTH HALL
THE BRITISH BILLIONAIRE'S INNOCENT BRIDE

THE MASTER OF HIGHBRIDGE MANOR

BY

SUSANNE JAMES

All the characters in this book have no existence outside the imagination of the author, and have no relation whatsoever to anyone bearing the same name or names. They are not even distantly inspired by any individual known or unknown to the author, and all the incidents are pure invention.

First published in Great Britain 2010
Harlequin Mills & Boon Limited,
Eton House, 18-24 Paradise Road, Richmond, Surrey TW9 1SR

© Susanne James 2010

ISBN: 978 0 263 87811 0

Harlequin Mills & Boon policy is to use papers that are natural, renewable and recyclable products and made from wood grown in sustainable forests. The logging and manufacturing process conform to the legal environmental regulations of the country of origin.

Printed and bound in Spain
by Litografia Rosés, S.A., Barcelona

THE MASTER OF HIGHBRIDGE MANOR

CHAPTER ONE

RIA drove slowly towards the entrance of the large Victorian building, the tyres of her elderly car grumbling along the gravel drive. A faint smile played around her lips as she took in the scene… This was the archetypal daunting place of learning, she thought, as she imagined the scores of pale-faced children who would have come to this boarding school for the first time, their stomachs churning, their mouths dry. Something she could easily identify with.

The school was a long two-storey building, its two sections separated by a bell tower and, although it had obviously stood for a hundred years or more in this rather remote area of the Hampshire countryside, it looked well-maintained and cared-for. The lawns flanking the drive were neat and orderly, with white stones placed at regular intervals along the edge to prohibit the unauthorized parking of cars, and over to the left were the four tennis courts, their nets taut and bristling with the anticipation of four hundred boys coming back for the start of the summer term.

A rush of familiarity filled Ria as she parked a little way away from the pillared-stone entrance and got out of the car. She had spent so much of her own childhood in a boarding school and, although she'd not yet set foot inside Highbridge

Manor, she knew it would present her with nothing new. There would be the smell of cleaning materials and polished wood, the distinctive dusty scent of books and paper, and somewhere from away in the distance the unmistakable odour of vegetables being boiled. Not that she would expect there to be any sign of cooking today, she realized, as she reached up to pull the doorbell, because the students were not due to return until next week.

As the heavy door was opened, Ria found herself looking up into the shrewd blue eyes of a smartly dressed woman in a grey skirt and jumper, her reading spectacles pushed up and planted safely on the top of her slightly greying brown hair. Ria instinctively guessed her to be about fifty, her self-assured manner demonstrating a comfortable familiarity with the place.

'Ah—Ria Davidson?' The woman's smile was strangely wary, and Ria answered quickly.

'Yes. I've an appointment with Mr Trent at ten-thirty,' she said.

There was a pause. 'We've been expecting you. Do come in.' She gestured for Ria to enter. 'I'm Helen Brown. I'm the school secretary,' she added.

Of course you are, Ria thought. You couldn't be anything else. In her experience, school secretaries were a breed apart—competent, possessive…and scary.

Ria followed Helen along the corridor and into a small room which overlooked the tennis courts.

'This is my abode, my study,' Helen said. 'Do sit down for a moment. I'll let Mr Trent know you're here.' She picked up the phone and dialled an internal number. 'Miss Davidson has arrived,' she murmured. 'Shall I bring her along now?' Then, 'Oh, yes, OK—we'll be with you in ten minutes.'

Glancing at the small clock on the wall in front of her, Ria noticed that it was still only ten-twenty—she'd arrived rather early. But, clearly, Mr Trent was sticking to the arrangement, she thought. Ten-thirty was ten-thirty—not ten-twenty! She sighed inwardly. He was going to be one of those, she thought—a stickler for precise detail.

Helen replaced the receiver. 'He's caught up with the care-taker at the moment,' she said. 'But he won't be long.'

Ria sat back, glad of a brief opportunity to find out a few things. 'The agency only contacted me yesterday about this position,' she began, and Helen interrupted.

'I know; it's been an absolute pain.' She paused. 'One of our English tutors left very unexpectedly just before the end of last term—which was somewhat unfortunate, but frankly…' and, speaking slightly from the corner of her mouth as if she might be overheard, Helen added, '…it was some-thing of a blessing in disguise. No tears shed, I can tell you.' She sighed. 'We've already interviewed three candidates, only one of whom was suitable—and she turned us down! So, we're in a bit of a fix at the moment.'

'Yes, I gathered this was a rush job.' Ria smiled.

'It's only a temporary post until the end of next term, in any case—as you know, I'm sure,' Helen went on. 'It should be easier to find someone permanent for September.'

'Have you been here a long time?' Ria asked Helen.

The woman smiled, studying her well-kept nails for a second. 'About fifteen years,' she said, 'so I feel I've earned my apprenticeship!'

'I understand it's always been a private school,' Ria said.

'Oh, yes—owned and run, very successfully, by the Trent family for as long as the school has been in existence,' Helen said. 'Which I think is quite a record of continuity, don't you?'

Presently, Helen stood up. 'I think we can go now,' she said, glancing up at the clock. It was exactly ten twenty-eight.

They walked together along the polished floor of the long

corridor, arriving at a door at the end which stated 'Head-master' in bold lettering. Helen knocked timidly and waited and, after a moment, a strong voice answered, 'Come.'

As she followed Helen inside, Ria had to shade her eyes against the strong sunlight which shafted in through the windows, but as she quickly adjusted her vision she was almost bowled over by the awesome vision of Mr Jasper Trent.

He was *young*—not old at all—which she'd thought he would be, probably only in his late thirties, and was six feet four at least, she guessed, broad-shouldered and well-built, and dressed formally in a dark suit and tie. His black hair was fashionably cut, his strong, bold features dominated by the most all-seeing dark eyes Ria had ever seen in her life. My goodness, she thought; there wouldn't be any problem with discipline in this school! Would anyone like to argue with Mr Jasper Trent? And, when he spoke, his crisp, authoritative voice answered that question!

'Miss Davidson? Please come in and sit down,' he said, the rather solemn features breaking into a brief smile as he came towards Ria. He held out his hand in greeting, clasping hers tightly. Then, 'Thank you, Helen.'

'Thank you, Mr Trent,' Helen said deferentially as she went out, closing the door softly behind her.

Trying hard to quell the anxious fluttering of her heart, Ria sat down on the large leather swivel chair she was offered, while Mr Trent took his own place behind the desk opposite and studied the latest candidate for the post on offer, his un-blinking gaze holding Ria almost spellbound.

Two immediate thoughts arose in his mind as he contin-ued looking at her—the first being one of undeniable en-chantment, very closely followed by one of intense irritation. This woman was not at all what he had expected, and he frowned, glancing down at the papers in front of him.

'You will forgive me for beginning by mentioning your age, Miss Davidson,' he said coolly, 'but I understood you to be…um…fifty-five years old.' He paused. 'Which, clearly, you are not.'

Ria couldn't help smiling—they'd both got something wrong this morning. 'No,' she agreed. 'I am twenty-five.'

'Well, that's something we've cleared up straight away,' Mr Trent said flatly and, noting the somewhat discouraging expression on his handsome features, Ria automatically held on to the arms of her chair to stop her hands from shaking. She'd always loathed interviews—and today's was no exception. Someone might have warned her what—who—to expect! Why had she thought he'd be a kind, fatherly person with grey hair and glasses and a body showing signs of wear and tear?

'So,' he went on, 'Miss Davidson is—twenty-five—and according to the CV which was e-mailed through to me yesterday, you're a graduate in English, with three years' teaching experience, together with supply work and some private tutoring…?'

'Correct,' Ria said.

'And you do realize that—if we find each other suitable—the position is only until the end of the present school year?' Mr Trent went on, his mind rushing ahead as usual. It might have been for longer than that if she proved to be the perfect applicant, he thought, but all his instincts told him that he shouldn't consider the possibility. Miss Ria Davidson was not only young, she was exquisite. Immaculately turned out in a cream linen suit, her rich auburn hair was coiled up on top and held with a tortoiseshell clip, while her fine buttermilk skin was flawless, her large hazel eyes set in whites of pure snow. Just the sort of woman he did not want on the premises, he told himself emphatically. For all sorts of reasons. He silently cursed the incompetence of the agency which had got her details wrong.

'I do realize that,' Ria said in answer to his question. 'And it fits my own plans exactly…*if* we find each other suitable,' she amended solemnly.

He raised one eyebrow. 'Am I allowed to know what your plans are?' he asked, and Ria shrugged.

'Oh, they aren't particularly original, I'm afraid,' she said. 'It's just that I have been enmeshed with school life from the age of four, and I suddenly feel the need to escape. So—' she paused '—in September I intend to travel to as many unusual destinations as I can. I have saved up enough to fund myself for about a year, but I'm sure I'll be able to find teaching work along the way—if I get desperate.' She paused. 'I don't want to leave it any longer or I'll lose my nerve.'

'Will you go alone?' Mr Trent enquired, his gaze flickering briefly at her long slender legs crossed neatly there in front of him.

'Yes, because unfortunately none of my friends can afford to have the time off,' Ria said, 'so I shall have to pluck up my courage. Anyway,' she added, 'I expect to meet plenty of ordinary people like me, doing the same thing.'

Several moments passed, during which he appeared to be deep in thought, before he spoke again.

'You would be required to teach the younger boys,' he said, 'and to complete the course already set for them. The Head of Department—Tim Robbinson—would give you full support, naturally.'

Looking back at him steadily, Ria had the impression that the job was as good as hers…if she wanted it. And she couldn't deny that she did want it!

'If our salary scale was not acceptable, I imagine that you wouldn't have come here today,' he said, glancing down and moving some papers on his desk, and Ria was painfully aware of his strong brown hands and long sensitive fingers.

'No—I mean, yes—your terms are...acceptable,' she said quickly.

There was another long pause, then, 'So...then I'm happy to offer you the post, Miss Davidson,' he said slowly, putting down the pen he'd been holding and leaning back in his chair. 'And, if you accept, I am sure you have some questions of your own.'

Ria felt a rush of exhilaration. She'd made it! And, even if it was only to be a very temporary position, it didn't alter the fact that she'd succeeded. Succeeded in convincing the head of this school that she was worth paying. For the first time during their meeting, Ria felt able to relax and give him the benefit of one of her dazzling smiles.

'Thank you—and I am pleased to agree,' she said lightly, adding, 'The agency gave me one of your brochures, so I don't think I need to ask you anything—at the moment,' she added slowly. Now that she was coming here, she thought, she'd take more time to really study the literature regarding this well-established place.

He stood up then, obviously relieved that the matter was settled. 'I'd better show you your accommodation,' he said. 'The caretaker has been making sure it's up to scratch.'

The main thing which had attracted Ria to the post was the fact that a room went with the job, because at the moment she had nowhere of her own in which to live. The lease on the flat she'd shared with her friend Sara had expired, and Sara was about to be married in any case. So, for the moment, the only valid address which Ria had was the parental family home in north London and, although she had her own space there if she needed it, it had never seemed like home. Why should it? She'd spent so little time there. And now, with Diana, her father's second wife, in control, it seemed less like home than ever.

Mr Trent opened the door for her to go in front of him, then they left the room and walked side by side along the corridor. He glanced down at her, noting the way that the sun's rays were adding golden lights to the glossiness of her hair.

'The place is obviously very quiet when the kids are away,' he remarked, trying to ignore the physical sensations rippling through his body at her closeness. 'But I try to make the most of it because a lot of noise goes with the job, I'm afraid. This time next week it'll be a very different matter.' He steered her around a corner at the far end of the corridor and they began mounting a wide stone staircase.

'I think anyone who's been in teaching, even for five minutes, would be impervious to noise and mayhem,' she said. She paused. 'But I've never worked at an all-boys boarding school before, so maybe I will have to ask for some advice now and then.' She looked up to find him staring down at her thoughtfully, and Ria coloured up immediately. She hoped that didn't make her sound pathetic. She swallowed. 'But I'm sure I'll soon fit in…' she added.

He nodded briefly. 'Everyone needs advice from time to time,' he said.

No more was said, and in a moment or two he unlocked a door at the end of the row and, going inside, Ria gazed around her, not believing her luck. This was not just a room—it was a small, well-contained flat! She followed Mr Trent as he showed her the tiny sitting room containing two armchairs and a round coffee table, a desk, bookcase and television set and, slightly cut off in one corner, what passed for a kitchen. It had a minute sink, a neat fridge, a kettle and a toaster and a microwave. It was just perfect for one person to eat casually, she thought, already sensing that she would feel at home here. The en suite bathroom adjoining the compact bedroom was the finishing touch. And she was going to have the place all to herself! What more did anyone need? She looked up gratefully.

'This is lovely,' she said. 'Far nicer than I expected,' she added truthfully, and he shrugged.

'It's very important for the staff to feel comfortable while they're working here,' he said. 'By the way, as a general rule, the staff have their main evening meal together in the dining room, but it's entirely up to you. Sometimes you may have work to complete and would prefer to eat alone in your room—which is why there are basic facilities here.'

'Do all the staff live in?' Ria asked, wandering over to the window to admire the tranquil view.

'No—only about half of them, I suppose,' he replied. 'The rest live close enough to do the daily commute.'

Presently, they made their way back downstairs and Mr Trent accompanied Ria to the entrance door, just as Helen emerged from her room.

'Ah, Helen—Miss Davidson will be taking up her post next week,' he said, and the woman smiled a rather strange little smile.

'Oh, good,' she said, and Ria looked at her quickly. She didn't know quite what to make of Helen Brown—was she friend…or foe? Too early to tell, she thought.

'I'll sort out all the formal stuff with the agency,' Helen said primly, going back into her room.

Outside, it was pleasantly warm as the two made their way to Ria's car, and she looked longingly at the tennis courts. She'd love a game now, she thought—to get some air into her lungs and to clear her head, which had felt distinctly dizzy since meeting Mr Trent.

Holding the car door open for her, he said, 'Do you have far to go? I don't think I was told where you live…'

'Actually, I'm homeless at the moment,' Ria said lightly.

'But a friend has been putting me up at her house in Salisbury for a few days.' She smiled. 'I expect she'll be quite glad to know that I've got somewhere else to live for a bit.'

She looked up uncertainly. He didn't seem in any hurry to go, but just stood there, leaning his arm on the open car door, his other hand thrust casually in his pocket.

'So,' he said, 'are you going back to Salisbury straight away?'

'Um…I don't know. I haven't really decided,' Ria said. She hadn't thought further than the morning's interview.

'Well, perhaps we'd better have some lunch,' he said. 'There are several decent places around here, and you'll need to get to know the area.'

That was the most unexpected invitation she'd had in a long time! And, after she was about to graciously refuse—this man was going to be her boss, after all; she didn't want to get too cosy!—something made Ria change her mind.

'Well…thanks,' she said simply. 'That's…very kind. Thank you,' she repeated.

He did stand back then. 'Hop out,' he said briefly. 'We'll take my car.'

Ria did as she was told, closing and locking her car door, and falling into step alongside him as they made their way towards the side of the building to where he obviously kept his car.

'By the way,' he said, glancing down at her, 'we always use Christian names at school—other than in the children's hearing. I'm Jasper. Which I expect you already know.'

Ria returned his glance. 'And, as *you* already know, I'm Ria,' she said lightly.

As they walked along in comparative silence, Jasper Trent sighed inwardly. He had expected to be confronted by a mature, no-nonsense woman this morning, not this perfect example of desirable womanhood.

Suddenly, he was desperate to get away from here and

hand the baton back to his brother—and resume his own profession. When Carl had asked this unexpected favour of him, he'd tried to come up with all sorts of reasons to refuse—one of which was that he doubted that he would really fit in here. Carl was such an outstanding headmaster that he, Jasper, would surely turn out to be a very pale imitation—even if it was to be a temporary arrangement. But eventually his sense of fair play had made him agree. It was Carl who'd been the dutiful son, after all—he deserved some quality time for himself. Because, although Jasper's Cambridge science degree had more than qualified him to teach, and to take a full part in the running of the school, he'd always declared his intention to do other things—to the huge disappointment of his father, who had expected both his sons to fall in line. To the older man, tradition was all. But then, as Jasper had pointed out on more than one occasion, every family had a black sheep, a rebel, and he was quite happy to fill that vacancy.

And now, watching the two from her window as they disappeared from her view, Helen Brown pursed her lips thoughtfully, then shrugged. Well, be it on his own head, she thought.

CHAPTER TWO

AS SHE sat beside him, her hands clasped in her lap, Ria couldn't help comparing the car she was sitting in with its owner—long, sleek and powerful. She glanced up at him, noticing for the first time—now that she was close to him— a faint but discernible mark running from the corner of his left eye and ending just short of his lip. He'd obviously been in an accident of some sort, she thought briefly, but nature had done a very good repair job because the scar did nothing at all to detract from his impossibly good looks. In fact, it seemed to add to his rugged appeal—an appeal which might even have hinted at cruelty…though Ria discounted that possibility straight away. Nothing about Jasper Trent, so far, suggested unkindness, or harshness. Anyway, she'd find out soon enough what he was *really* like—though she somehow didn't think their paths would cross much during the working day, sensing that he probably enjoyed a typically isolated position in his rather austere headmaster's room.

Being in the company of yet another handsome man made Ria's thoughts turn briefly to Seth… Would she ever be able to banish him entirely from her mind? she asked herself. But how *could* she easily rub out that time when her heart had been ripped from her? As if it was some minor incident that could be forgotten? And was the man sitting beside her another one just like him—was he, too, utterly self-confident, utterly self-assured, delighting in his powerful masculinity? Did Jasper Trent see only his own life and hopes and dreams—with scant concern for anyone else's?

She turned her attention to the scenery unfolding all around them and took a deep breath. She had no doubt that Jasper Trent had been in perfect charge of his school for a good number of years, running it with impeccable authority. But what did he do in his private life? she wondered. To her, he didn't look the marrying kind with a clutch of kids at home, so how would he spend his time, what did he do in order to relax? Ria scolded herself. What he did or didn't do was no concern of hers.

He glanced across at her briefly. 'You'll have noticed the car parking area when we picked mine up just now,' he said. 'You might even be lucky enough to nab one of the garages sometimes.'

Ria smiled. 'Oh, my car has never been used to the dignity of being garaged,' she said. 'Anyway, I'll be selling it in a few months' time when I head off.' She paused. 'And, who knows…I may not come back at all. I may find that the grass really is greener away from England.'

'There's only one way to find out about that,' he said levelly, keeping his eyes on the road ahead.

'It'll do me good to put my toe into alien waters and see if I can cope with the unknown without going to pieces,' Ria said. She wasn't going to admit that she was already rather dreading the moment of departure, that sometimes she wished she'd never planned it at all. But she'd talked for hours and hours with friends who'd done exciting things, been to exciting places, and she'd boxed herself into a corner she couldn't escape from. And everyone was egging her on all the time—to change her mind now would be pathetic.

The Lamb was about a five-minute drive from the school, and the restaurant was just nicely crowded as, presently, Ria and her new employer sat at a corner table by the window enjoying their meal. She looked across at him as she put down her knife.

'That cheese platter was just perfect,' she said. 'Thank you.'

He leaned back and picked up his pint of lager. 'Yes, the food is generally pretty good here,' he said, 'and the atmosphere is always relaxed and congenial. It seems to have become the school's "local" over the years. Some of the staff drop in for a drink now and then, and our older pupils, too, have been known to enjoy chilling out after exams.' He watched as Ria drank the last of the sparkling water she'd ordered, noting the way her slender fingers curled around the stem of the glass, admiring the unassuming elegance of her every move. She looked up then and saw him studying her, and almost at once her cool cheeks warmed visibly.

'So,' she said lightly, 'term begins next Wednesday—a week from today?'

'It does,' he replied. 'But the boys will be returning on Monday—or some on Tuesday.' He paused. 'I expect you'd like to do the same?'

'Tuesday would be very convenient for me,' Ria said.

'Helen will be at school permanently from Monday. She'll give you your keys, show you the ropes.'

'Does Helen live in?' Ria asked.

'No, she has a cottage just walking distance from school. She lives there with her elderly mother,' he replied briefly.

'She seems very…competent,' Ria said.

He replied quickly, 'She is certainly that. I think we're all a bit afraid of her.'

Ria smiled, but said nothing. She could never imagine Jasper Trent being afraid of anyone—or anything.

'And do you live permanently "above the shop"?' Ria

asked innocently, hoping that she wasn't being inquisitive—but wanting to know, just the same.

'I occupy my own flat during most of term time,' he replied casually, 'but it's not my permanent home.' He paused before going on, 'I am merely acting Head of school, in any case,' he added shortly.

Ria looked across, really surprised at that. 'Oh?' she said curiously.

'My brother is the permanent Head, but he decided he'd like a bit of time off, so I agreed to step into his shoes for a few months and allow him some space.' The strong mouth lifted wryly in one corner as he went on, 'But, unfortunately, while he was on a skiing trip he had a bad accident, resulting in various complications, so the anticipated few months will have become a full school year.' He cleared his throat. 'But he takes up the reins again in September.'

Ria couldn't help feeling confused. Jasper Trent had seemed to her to be the perfect headmaster, determined and authoritative, and apparently entrenched in the school's life. She decided to go one step further.

'So…where do you normally live, then?' she asked.

'Somerset,' he said briefly. 'Not so far away that I can't make fairly regular flying visits for a day or so when I feel like it.'

Yes, but what did he do in Somerset? Ria wondered—but didn't have the courage to enquire, and neither spoke for a few moments after that.

'You said you were "homeless" at the moment,' Jasper said casually.

'Well, that's not exactly true,' she said. 'My family home is in north London, but I've hardly ever lived there, not really. Though, naturally, I was sometimes there in the school holidays. But the house is often empty because my father works for the Foreign Office, and he and my stepmother are frequently away. So, until two months ago, I shared a flat with a girl friend, but her plans have changed so we didn't renew the lease and I feel in a bit of a vacuum at the moment.' She smiled. 'Luckily for me, the friend in Salisbury insisted I stay with her until I take off in September—but now, of course, thanks to Highbridge Manor, I shall have somewhere of my very own for a while.'

He'd been watching her closely as she spoke, loving the changing expressions flickering across her heart-shaped face, and every instinct he possessed warned him not to get carried away, not to be overly affected by this beautiful, warm and appealing woman. But Jasper Trent's more sensible instincts were heavily outnumbered by his hormones, and he was having difficulty keeping his eyes off her.

Pushing back his chair slightly, he glanced across. 'Let's order coffee, shall we? I could do with one.' Almost before she could agree or not, he'd got up and gone over to the bar. Ria watched him speaking briefly to the bartender. Jasper Trent was so outstandingly handsome, she thought—there must surely be a woman on the scene? How could he possibly avoid it? Yet nothing he'd said indicated that there was. It had all been very first person singular. Then her expression darkened briefly. He was probably—no, *obviously*—a man who enjoyed relationships with no ties. That must be it. With his physical attributes, he could pick from any bunch he happened to be with, enjoy the moment and pass on to the next. Then she bit her lip. *Stop it,* she told herself fiercely, stop putting the poor bloke in the compartment of your own choice. You know nothing of his personal life at all. Stop making things up.

In a few moments he returned to the table with a tray holding two mugs of coffee, plus a bowl of sugar and a small jug of cream, and she glanced up at him as he set the things down.

'You must have guessed how I like my coffee,' she murmured, helping herself to the sugar before letting a generous slick of cream dribble over the back of her spoon.

'Well, I knew you probably wouldn't like it the way I do,' he said easily, picking up his own black unsweetened coffee. 'And, since I don't know your particular tastes, I thought I'd cover all possibilities.'

She smiled now as she put the mug to her lips. 'And you got it just right,' she said.

His black eyes softened as he continued gazing at her. And he wasn't alone in his fascination. He'd been only too aware of the lingering glances in her direction from other males in the restaurant—and the man behind the bar, who knew the residents of Highbridge Manor very well, had been blunt enough to enquire who she was. 'New girl on the block?' he'd asked suggestively, raising his eyes in appreciation. And Jasper had fielded the question casually, as if he was surprised at the enquiry. 'Oh, yes, but very temporary—she's sort of passing through,' he'd said, turning away with the drinks.

Presently, glancing at his watch, Jasper said, 'I'm sorry to rush you but I'm interviewing a part-time games assistant at three o'clock…'

Ria immediately got to her feet. 'Of course, and I should be getting along,' she said. 'I told Hannah that I'd be back long before this.' She bent to pick up her bag. 'It's her birthday today,' she added, 'and we're going out somewhere later to celebrate.' She looked up at Jasper as he stood aside to let her go past. 'It'll be a double celebration,' she added, 'because I've got a job with a home attached.'

Much later, after he'd finished what he had to do, Jasper shut down his computer, then picked up his jacket from the back of the chair. It had been a good day, he thought, all the important details connected with the start of his last term successfully completed. The young games assistant he'd appointed seemed able and enthusiastic, and it had been a great relief to have found someone to fill the temporary post in the English department. He paused for a moment before leaving the room, a slight frown creasing his brow. He hoped he'd done the right thing, engaging Ria Davidson... It wasn't anything to do with her ability in her subject, of course, and he knew only too well that his pupils would fall for her at first sight—but would she be able to keep them in their place? Keep law and order in the classroom? Yet something told him that she'd cope well enough and, anyway, *he'd* make damned sure the boys wouldn't take advantage of her. He had a daunting reputation for looking in briefly—unexpectedly—while classes were in progress, to check up on general discipline, and nothing ever escaped his notice. He took pleasure in running a tight ship, so it would be in his own interests to steer Miss Davidson through any troubled waters for the short time she'd be at the school.

For some reason, Jasper felt strangely restless. Perhaps he'd go home tonight, rather than wait until the weekend as he'd intended. His beautiful old cottage in the countryside frequently enticed him back, and today was one of those days. Besides, he might not be able to be there very much during the frantically busy summer term ahead—the end-of-year examinations, and the end of his tenure. Speech day, final cricket matches and the tennis tournament to arrange... School-leavers' functions and presentations. It all added up to a mass of organization which must be sorted by him. It was obvious he wouldn't have much time for himself, so he'd better escape for a few days now, while he had the chance.

After telling the caretaker that he was about to leave, he made his way over to the car park. Allowing for traffic, he'd be home in time for supper. He'd phone Debra and tell her he was coming. He knew she didn't like it when he was away for too long at a time.

Ria and Hannah left the cosy trattoria where they'd spent the evening and strolled along the streets of the town, gazing in at the brightly lit shop windows.

'I feel really lucky getting that job,' Ria said, 'because I need the money to top up my resources for next year. Not to mention having somewhere to live! Couldn't be more convenient.'

'I think they're lucky to get *you*,' Hannah said, 'and don't forget—you're always welcome to stay at mine again, if things don't turn out right. Although,' she added mischievously, 'from your description of Mr Headmaster, I doubt whether you'll give up on the place—or on him—very quickly.'

'It will certainly be in my interests *not* to give up,' Ria said firmly, 'however bad or difficult things turn out to be. Anyway, it's to be for such a short time.' They waited for some cars to pass before crossing the road. 'And, by the way, Hannah, please don't let your romantic imagination run away with you, *please*. You know very well what my feelings are in that direction.'

Hannah stopped and took hold of Ria's arm for a second. 'When are you going to give yourself a break and get back to normal, Ria?' she asked seriously. 'This state of affairs isn't right. You've got to start believing in yourself again, and get rid of all that guilt you're carrying around with you. You deserve to find happiness with someone else.'

'If you say so, Hannah,' Ria replied listlessly, 'but at the moment all I require, all I care about, is a job and somewhere of my own to rest my head. And, thanks to Mr Jasper Trent, I've got both.'

CHAPTER THREE

ON THE following Tuesday afternoon, Ria stood in the centre of her new bedroom and looked around. With her own duvet and pillows cosily in place and her make-up, travel clock and other personal belongings neatly arranged on the small table by her bed, it was already beginning to feel like home.

Ria always managed to travel fairly light, her clothes packed into two suitcases, with a couple of large holdalls coping with other bulkier stuff, and it hadn't taken her long to unpack. The one wardrobe and chest of drawers were perfectly adequate to hold the modest amount of clothing she'd brought with her—which mostly consisted of simple things suitable for the classroom.

Going into the bathroom, she swilled her hands and face and released her hair from its ponytail, feeling the need to relax for a few moments. She wouldn't mind having a quick nap, she thought wryly—she and Hannah had stayed up very late last night, talking, but apart from that Ria recognized the tremor of apprehension she always experienced in new situations. Surely she should be growing out of that by now? she scolded herself. She bit her lip thoughtfully. Her anticipated year of travelling was going to clinch it, once and for all, she thought.

Outside her room, Jasper Trent hesitated for a few seconds

before knocking on the door. He'd been told that she'd arrived but had deliberately not bothered to seek her out or make a particular point of welcoming her. Anyway, Helen would have taken care of her, taken care of everything.

Ever since he'd appointed Ria, he'd asked himself over and over again what on earth had made him do it. But then he'd been getting desperate about filling the post, he'd reasoned, and she had impressed him—on so many counts. Although she was much younger than he'd have liked, she was direct in conversation, with no fluffy beating about the bush or being tongue-tied, and he had the feeling that she could state her case with no difficulty. Could take care of herself. Just as well, he thought, if she intended travelling alone in the not-too-distant future. Then he shrugged. That was a long way off and none of his concern. His only responsibility was in seeing that she did the job he'd be paying her for—and that she behaved herself. His expression hardened. He'd learned a strong lesson this year, learned it in spades. He'd be relieved when Carl took over again, he thought—the difficulties of the business world could be tricky enough, but running a large boarding school was in a category all of its own.

Now, he gave two short raps on Ria's door and, after a few moments, she opened it and stood aside at once for him to come in.

'Hi, there,' he said casually, glancing around him briefly. 'Just checking that you're here, and that everything's OK.'

She smiled up at him quickly. 'I am here, and everything's perfectly OK,' she said brightly. He was formally dressed as before, but he seemed even taller in the confined space of her small flat, and she was intensely conscious of his eyes searching her out as he gazed down. 'Helen gave me my key,' she said, 'and she also introduced me to Tim Robbinson.'

'Ah, yes, good… Tim is a very able head of department.

I'm sure you'll get on well. And if there are any problems
don't be afraid to ask him.' He paused. 'Or me, for that matter,'
he added as an afterthought. 'I don't want there to be any un-
finished business left for my brother to sort out when he
returns, and I naturally rely on all the staff to support me in
that aim.' He paused. 'What I don't know about, I can't deal
with,' he added.

Ria felt slightly confused for a moment. His attitude was
strangely cool today, she thought, lacking the easy familiarity
there'd been before. Still, what did she expect? That was then,
this was now. He was the boss—and she shouldn't forget it.

He stared down at her. The jeans and white T-shirt she was
wearing made her look younger, more vulnerable than when
she'd presented herself as the brisk, archetypal interviewee,
and her hair, loose like that around her shoulders, added to
the unsophisticated impression, to her appeal.

He cleared his throat. 'It's been bedlam here all day, of
course, with the boarders returning,' he said, 'and it won't be
much better tomorrow when the day boys come back.' He
went over to look out of the window for a second. 'But, by
Thursday, some work should be in progress and a modicum
of sanity restored.'

'Oh—I thought all the pupils were boarders,' Ria said, and
he interrupted.

'No, only about half of them. Their quarters are in the resi-
dential block over there—you can see it from this window—
while we, the staff, live here in the old, original building.' He
turned to look at her again, and Ria's heart missed a beat or
two. He had to be about the most gorgeous headmaster this
side of the equator, she thought. Good job he didn't run a girls'
school. They'd make his life impossible.

'I…I…um…would offer you a cup of tea,' she began, 'but
I haven't been to the shops yet, or sorted out my kitchen…'

'Thank you, but I don't need tea at the moment,' he said flatly. 'By the way, the basics should be here already—tea, and coffee et cetera, and when you need more you can ask Claudia, the housekeeper. She's in charge of all that kind of thing, but it's up to you how you stock your kitchen.' He turned to look at her again, trying to stem the feelings which would keep surfacing, conscious of a familiar, annoying muscle in his neck twitching briefly. There was silence for a few moments, then, without looking at her, he said, 'I believe Tim gave you the timetable and showed you the way around—where you're going to be teaching?' He didn't wait for her to reply before going on, 'I appreciate that it's a lot to take in all at once…'

'Oh, I'll probably cope,' Ria said.

'Yes, I'm sure you will,' he said, going towards the door. He turned to glance back at her. 'Helen told me that she's shown you where the dining room is—and dinner is at eight o'clock.'

As he went back down the staircase, Jasper frowned, cross with himself. The trouble was, he admitted to himself, he didn't feel particularly cool when he was in Ria Davidson's presence.

After he'd gone, Ria felt rattled. In two or three minutes flat, Jasper Trent had managed to really confuse her. He was so charming and considerate at the interview; now he was acting like a different person. Of course, then it had been in his interests to show her his nicer side because it had been obvious that he was having difficulty in filling the vacant post, and time was running out. But he'd got what he'd wanted and now he was fulfilling his allotted role here—master of the house in every sense.

She wandered over to the window and stared out for a few moments. She could see the boys' dormitory block quite easily from here—as Jasper had pointed out—and now the area was a hive of activity with boys and parents going in and out with cases and belongings.

She went across to the sink to fill the kettle. Jasper Trent might not feel the need for a cup of tea, she thought, but at this precise moment she was desperate for one.

Ria spent the rest of the afternoon arranging and rearranging her things in the flat and stacking her books into the bookcase. She always had study materials with her—dictionaries and reference books—but was never without a current novel to read before she settled down to sleep at the end of each day.

Later, glancing at the clock, she realized that it was time to get ready for dinner, so, after having a quick shower, she took out her straight, knee-length black pencil skirt and cream lacy top from the wardrobe, before tying her hair back in one long plait. There wouldn't be any need for much make-up, she thought wryly, because her cheeks were already rosy-pink with the anxious anticipation of having to mingle with a crowd of complete strangers who were already known to each other.

At about quarter to eight there was a discreet knock on the door and Ria's heart fluttered—much to her annoyance. Jasper Trent was no doubt presenting himself to accompany her down to the dining room, she thought, glancing once again in the mirror before going over to open the door. Perhaps he had some more instructions for her! But it was Helen, not Jasper, who was standing there.

'Everything OK? Settling in all right?' Helen enquired and, without waiting for a reply, said, 'I've come to fetch you because I thought you might like some company on your first evening—I'm staying for dinner myself, tonight.' She didn't bother to mention that she was following Jasper's instructions in accompanying Ria.

A wave of gratitude swept over Ria. She'd been dreading going into that crowded dining room by herself.

'Oh, thanks, Helen, that was thoughtful of you,' she said, picking up her bag. 'I'm all ready.'

'I don't always stay for dinner,' Helen remarked, as they went down the wide staircase, 'because I need to get back. I live with my mother, who often isn't well enough to do any cooking. But she's not too bad at the moment, so it won't matter if I'm late home.'

'What's the food like at Highbridge Manor?' Ria asked lightly as they walked along together. 'Edible?'

'You wait and see,' Helen replied as they approached the dining room, through the open doors of which loud conversation could be heard. 'Sandy is a fantastic chef, and all I need to add is that half the staff are overweight!'

As they went inside, Ria saw that three long trestle tables were laid for the meal, but everyone seemed to be standing around in groups, chatting, with drinks in their hands. Almost immediately, Jasper appeared at their side.

'Ladies,' he said formally, 'what would you like to drink? Helen, you like red wine, don't you—and, Ria, what can I get for you?'

Ria was about to say that all she wanted was some water, but that would sound so boring, she thought, so at the last second she said, 'Yes, I'd like red wine, too, please.'

In a few moments Jasper came back with their drinks and Ria looked up at him quickly. He was wearing grey well-cut trousers and an open-neck shirt which revealed his strong-muscled neck and throat. She'd already been aware that he was one of the tallest—if not *the* tallest—man in the room, his whole persona casting an aura of stylish dominance about him, and his voice—that voice which had barely left her consciousness for a week, and which could only be described as commanding of tone—carried easily above the hubbub of conversation in the room.

Helen moved away then to speak to someone for a moment, leaving Ria standing next to Jasper. Dragging her eyes away from him, she took a sip of her wine and glanced around, trying to get a handle on her surroundings. There were at least forty members of staff present, she noticed, mostly men, and she tried not to be aware of the glances directed at her by several of them, not responding to their unashamed interest. At the other end of the room she saw a long counter and open hatch from where their food was obviously served, and Jasper followed her gaze.

'I'm afraid we have to help ourselves to everything,' he said, looking down at her. 'Waiter service was abandoned long ago.' His eyes narrowed briefly. Ria Davidson did wear her clothes so well, he thought. The outfit she had on was simple enough, but she somehow managed to make it look outstanding. He smiled suddenly, disarmingly, and Ria smiled back, a welcome surge of pleasure filling her for a moment. He *was* nice, she thought instinctively. His attitude towards her earlier in the day was probably out of character... Well, she certainly hoped so.

'I'm not used to people waiting on me,' she said. 'And, anyway, I prefer to choose what I have to eat.'

Almost at once, someone struck a gong by the hatch and everyone moved forward straight away. Jasper put his hand lightly on Ria's arm to push her in front of him. 'That gong,' he said, 'has been in more or less constant use since the first day this school existed.'

She looked up at him, her eyes bright with interest. 'Really? The same one?' she said eagerly. 'I love that—it's history, isn't it?'

They took their places in the queue and she went on, 'I have an almost unhealthy liking for consistency, for maintaining things as they always were.' She paused. 'I don't think I like change, that's the thing, and sometimes I wish I could "stop all the clocks"—do you know Auden's poem?—"Stop all the clocks, Cut off the telephone, Prevent the dog from barking with a juicy bone, Silence the pianos and with muffled drum…" Oh, it goes on and on,' she said apologetically, 'but what I'm talking about is not being able to hold on to something you're enjoying…valuing…or on to good times, generally, I suppose. I mean…contentment with any situation often seems to slip through your fingers before you've had the chance to appreciate it.'

She looked up at him, colour instantly flooding her cheeks as their eyes met, and she shrank inside herself for a moment. What on earth had made her waffle on like that—and what must he think of her? 'I sometimes feel it would be good for everything to just pause…for a bit,' she added, her voice faltering for a second.

He didn't reply at once, enjoying listening to her… He had spotted the potential in Ria Davidson on their first meeting, he reminded himself. Apart from being a modern, fashionable woman, she was much deeper than her appearance might have suggested, and there was that beguiling thoughtfulness about her that sent his male urges tingling in a familiar way.

'I do know what you mean,' he said, 'about the manic passing of time—and I have a lot of sympathy with your outlook. In fact, I see my place in Somerset as the sanctuary I rely on to detach me from all the change and progress and stress you're talking about. Life, there, does actually seem to stand still sometimes.'

She looked up at him gratefully. Just so long as he didn't think she was crazy!

It was their turn to choose the food they wanted, and Ria was impressed by the variety on offer. There was delicious-looking chicken, coated in a fine honey glaze, tender pork fillet with onion stuffing, thick slices of baked ham with peach dressing, an interesting-looking vegetarian alternative, plus several different vegetables or salad to go with it all. She looked up at Jasper.

'How can I choose from all this?' she asked helplessly.

'The menu on our first day back is always rather self-indulgent,' he admitted, 'but we must make the most of it—it'll probably be mince and mash tomorrow!'

Helen was standing almost right behind them and she called out, 'See what I mean, Ria? It never takes much persuasion to get me to stay for dinner occasionally.'

There was apparently no pecking order at the tables, everyone sitting where they liked and, seated between Helen and Jasper, Ria suddenly felt so overwhelmingly optimistic she could have burst into tears. It must be that glass of wine making her feel so sensitive, she thought, or the tender pork she'd just finished, right to the last morsel. Whatever it was, she wasn't complaining and, when the glorious creamy desserts appeared at the counter, she felt as if she'd been invited to a wonderful celebration of some sort instead of her first night at her new job! She bit her lip—she hoped she wasn't going to turn into Cinderella and find that this was all a charade, a terrible mistake that she was here at all. Then she silently kicked herself. Why spoil the evening with these horrible, dark thoughts? Why couldn't she leave all that behind, once and for all? Was she never going to be able to believe that life could be good, happy and fulfilling once again?

The meal ended and they all stood up to leave just as Tim Robbinson sauntered across to speak to them. He was obviously younger than Jasper, Ria noted, his mass of brown curly hair framing a happy, uncomplicated face, reminding her of an oversized baby.

'Hi, everyone,' Tim said good-naturedly. 'That was a great meal, Jasper.'

Jasper nodded. 'Yes, it was.' He paused. 'Look, I've got a phone call to make,' he said. 'Perhaps you'd like to stay and have a few words with Ria, Tim. I'm sure there's plenty of stuff she wants to find out.'

'My pleasure,' Tim said at once, smiling at Ria, and for the next twenty minutes or so the two sat chatting together easily.

Presently, the room emptied and, after saying goodnight to Tim, Ria wandered out of the building, breathing in the balmy air gratefully. She didn't feel like going to bed yet because she wasn't at all tired, she realized—her head too full of everything that had gone on, so turning impulsively, she decided to go for a short walk.

She had spotted a small wooded area behind the tennis courts and, curious to know where it led, she set off, her feet treading lightly over the short grass. Almost immediately, she could see that the path led to the cricket green—the surroundings of this school were almost unbelievably beautiful, she thought, certainly outdoing anything *she'd* ever known.

It was nearly dark now, as Ria came to a small gate leading to some open ground where a small flock of sheep were grazing and, leaning over it, she wished that she could hold this perfect tranquil moment for ever. What a fantastic—and rather unusual—slice of luck had come her way, she thought, that the temporary post she'd been looking for had landed her here! Could this be the first small ray of hope that the ball might bounce in her direction?

As usual, Ria's introspectiveness threw the events of her life into sharp focus, once again, as she stood there…how different things might have been, she thought…if only. She certainly wouldn't be here at Highbridge Manor. She would be cradling her longed-for baby in her arms and basking in the warmth and love of a real family. A faint snort of derision left her lips. In her dreams, she thought bleakly.

Suddenly, and without any warning, her eyes filled and two large tears gently coursed down her cheeks. And she didn't try to stop them. It was good to cry, so she'd been told. So then, she'd cry. Well, she'd done enough of it in the last year. But it was strange that her feelings of happiness at being here could make her feel so sad.

'Oh, dear—we haven't upset you already, have we, Ria?'

Jasper had seen her walking away in the distance as he'd returned from parking the car and had decided to catch her up, to keep her company, admitting that something about her brought out all his protective instincts. Well, it was her first day, after all.

Nearly jumping out of her skin at the sound of his voice, Ria turned and looked up into those achingly desirable eyes, which were glistening more blackly than ever in the dim light, and she unzipped her bag, frantically searching for a tissue.

'Oh...no...I think it's a bit of hay fever, that's all,' she lied. 'I do suffer from it occasionally.'

Help, she thought. How did he know where I was—and why did he follow me, anyway? She was going to have to pull herself together and act normally.

She found a tissue, dabbing at her eyes. 'I was just admiring this wonderful place,' she sniffed. 'I hope the boys realize how lucky they are to be at school here.'

'Oh, I doubt it,' Jasper said flatly. 'Did any of us appreciate our lives when we were young? It's the norm to take everything for granted, isn't it?'

Well, the good life had certainly been the norm for him and Carl, he acknowledged, feeling a sense of shame when he compared their lot with some of the boys who turned up here. The Trent brothers had had loving and diligent parents, whose one thought had been the well-being and happiness of their sons—and of all the children who passed through their school.

Neither spoke for a moment, then Ria said, pointing, 'Does the school own all this land as well?'

'Yes—that's all part of us,' he said. 'Local farmers borrow it from time to time to feed their stock.' He paused. 'Observing those animals, hearing them grazing, pulling lazily at the grass, especially after the sun's gone down, can be very therapeutic,' he added, and Ria glanced up at him quickly. He had expressed her own inner thoughts exactly.

He was standing very close to her now, so that they were almost touching, and for a ridiculous moment Ria wanted to lean into him, to feel the warmth of his body mingle with hers, to be comforted, to be loved. It must be wonderful to be the woman in his life, she thought—because there *had* to be one. There had to be a beautiful woman somewhere, waiting for this gorgeous, strong, dependable man to come home, she thought and, to her horror, Ria thought she was going to start crying again. But feeling sorry for herself was the last thing she could do with right now.

Moving away from him slightly, she blew her nose.

'So, then, won't you be sorry to leave all this when your brother comes back?' she asked.

'Oh…sort of…I suppose,' he said non-committally. 'But Carl is the one for this job, not me—not really. No, he is the headmaster par excellence.'

Something in the faintly sardonic tone of Jasper's voice as he said that made Ria frown briefly. She was in no doubt that Jasper Trent had fulfilled his obligations to perfection during the short time he'd been in office. In fact, Tim had said as much, earlier. 'Jasper has been terrific,' he'd said, 'and great to work with, so long as you watch your Ps and Qs…though he doesn't suffer fools gladly. Which is why he's so successful with the manufacturing business he owns in Somerset, I suppose,' he'd added. 'Everyone certainly knows exactly where they stand with him.'

Now, not really wanting to leave this spot, yet realizing that it was getting late, Ria turned to leave. 'I suppose I should go back—and have a good night's sleep,' she said, glancing up and forcing herself to smile quickly at Jasper as he fell into step beside her.

He looked down at her thoughtfully. As soon as he'd reached her a few minutes ago, he'd known only too well that she was upset about something. And it had been nothing at all to do with hay fever, either. That season had not arrived yet. No, he sensed Ria Davidson to be far more vulnerable than the impression she liked to give—perhaps partly explained by the fact that she had spent so much of her childhood away from her family, he thought. She had also mentioned her stepmother briefly, hadn't she. Perhaps they had never got on, and she still nurtured bad memories. But all that was unlikely to be the cause of her distress tonight, he reasoned. He hoped she wasn't regretting accepting the post, regretting being here. Yet he knew that wasn't the case. She had been so obviously grateful to have her own flat, and to earn the money which would help her get started on her travels, and during dinner she'd been lively and quite obviously feeling happy.

He shrugged inwardly. Keeping the staff contented with their lot, sorting out emotional and practical problems with everyone from time to time, had been one of the most difficult aspects of the job and Carl was welcome to have it back, he thought.

They walked back together in comparative—but surprisingly easy—silence, and by now it was almost pitch-black. But the security lights everywhere were more than sufficient to light up their path as they returned to the school building.

'I'm just going back to my car for a moment,' Ria said. 'Something I've forgotten.'

'I've forgotten something, too,' he said, looking down and smiling briefly.

They made their way to the far side of the building towards the car park, Ria hugging her bare arms because, despite the warmth of the day, the night air had a distinctly chilly feel about it. Opening her car door, she reached over to the glovebox where she'd left the novel she was presently reading. It was by one of her favourite authors and Ria was glad that she'd remembered she'd left it behind. A few chapters later would relax her and give her what she hoped would be a restful night.

As she walked back slowly, Jasper was slamming his door and he looked up as she came up to him.

'I'd forgotten my book,' Ria said, trying to hide it under her arm. She didn't imagine that her current choice of bedtime reading would meet with the headmaster's approval!

'And I'd forgotten my jacket,' he remarked, slinging it casually over one shoulder.

'Well, I wish I'd remembered to bring mine because it's not quite summer yet, is it?' she began and, before she could think—or say—another word, she found her shoulders being covered by Jasper's jacket as he wrapped it around her.

'There—that had to be the reason why I forgot to take this with me earlier,' he said, and at his touch Ria's whole body trembled—with what? she asked herself desperately. Not with *desire*, surely! Her tongue went dry at the thought. Hadn't desire, as far as she was concerned, been extinguished for ever? And, if it hadn't, would she ever let it put her at risk again? She quickened her step, going slightly ahead of him for a second, wanting to put space between them.

'Well, that was lucky for me, then,' she said, needing to get back to the sanctity and privacy of her room. 'Thank you…Jasper.' Did her voice sound as tremulous to him as it did to her?

They returned to the building and Jasper paused for a moment, looking down at her. 'Well, then…classes start in earnest on Thursday,' he said. 'Tim will be looking after you.'

'Yes, thanks—he's already spoken to me about the last bit of the course we've got to cover,' Ria said, turning away. 'Goodnight, then…'

'Goodnight, Ria,' he said slowly. 'By the way,' he began, and there was a pause as she glanced back at him questioningly. 'Um…my jacket?' he suggested mildly, and Ria gasped, slipping it from her shoulders.

'Of course! I'm so sorry… I'd forgotten about it—it felt so…cosy,' she said, blushing. *How* could she have forgotten she had on something that was about ten sizes too big for her?

As he took it from her, her book fell to the floor and he immediately stooped to retrieve it. He glanced at the cover before handing it back to her without comment, and Ria's heart sank. Why couldn't it have been her copy of *War and Peace* instead of the colourful romantic novel she was enjoying?

They parted company and, after making his normal, late-night check-up and speaking to the caretaker, Jasper went back to his own flat, which was four away from the one Ria was occupying. As he passed her door, he imagined her slipping out of her clothes, perhaps already soaping her delectable figure under the shower, letting the water caress her creamy skin…

As he shut his door—with an unnecessarily firm bang—he cursed himself volubly. He was a hopeless case, he told himself grimly, because he knew he was in danger of being emotionally trapped yet again—big time. He had enjoyed the company of too many beautiful women in his life, admitting that he'd taken his time in choosing the one he would eventually select as his wife…and what a bloody nose she'd given him! Why wasn't he more like Carl, who never seemed to need a woman?

Carl seemed happy and content to focus entirely on his career, on this school and its continuing status and success.

Jasper stared moodily in the mirror, his eyes gleaming with dark intensity as his thoughts ran on. Then he turned resolutely. This latest female to stir his masculine propensities would be gone out of his sight for ever in a matter of months—and, until then, he'd make sure he had as little to do with her as was humanly possible. It was imperative—vital—for him to keep his mind, his thoughts, fixed on his responsibilities here, for this final term. Surely he could manage that.

As he went to hang up his jacket, the faintest drift of Ria's perfume, still lingering in the fabric, reached his nostrils and he clicked his tongue in annoyance. *That* didn't help! Next time—perhaps every time—that he wore it, she would be right there close to him, taunting him, teasing him, without even realizing it.

CHAPTER FOUR

ALMOST four weeks into her job, and Ria had hardly seen Jasper at all. He never attended the morning assemblies, and only on two occasions had she seen him in the distance, surrounded by a group of older boys. But the distinctive voice could be heard above the general hubbub, and on that occasion it was obvious that he was making an important point! Ria had smiled to herself. There had never been any doubt in her mind who was in charge here, and the fact that he was seldom seen—leaving the day-to-day teaching to his staff—added to his quietly aloof stature.

She was relieved that she had been allowed to get through these first days without being hassled or checked-up on. So far, she'd only been asked to teach the twelve-year-old boys and she found them cooperative and well-behaved and, although she admitted to feeling dead tired by the time her duties ended at four-thirty, it was a happy and satisfying tiredness. She felt she was coping OK, and Tim had only looked in on two of her lessons, and had later given her the thumbs-up sign as they'd passed in the corridor. She had the impression that she was being trusted to do her job properly without undue interference.

The only social occasion seemed to be the evening meal,

which was more like a running buffet, with people coming and going at different times. But it did give Ria some time to meet other members of staff and have a chat for an hour. Jasper had certainly not been seen in the dining room since that first Tuesday, so he either came down much later, Ria thought, or didn't bother at all. Or maybe he preferred to eat his dinner alone in his room, or in the pub they'd been to. Anyway, it didn't matter to her. She was glad not to see him. She was enjoying her life, so far, and one of the best bits of it was closing her door and being by herself in her own flat, to make some tea and sometimes to watch late evening television.

One morning, a type-written note had been slipped under her door. It read:

There will be a staff meeting in the headmaster's room
at 5.30 today. Please do your best to attend.

It was obviously a circular, delivered by Helen, and was probably a regular event, Ria thought as she read it again. Jasper Trent keeping a firm hand on the steering wheel, keeping everyone on their toes.

After she'd finished lessons for the day, Ria let herself into her flat. Taking a fresh top from the wardrobe, she went into the bathroom for a quick shower before going down to the meeting. There wouldn't be time to wash her hair because it always took so long to dry, so she'd just have to pat it into place for now, she thought.

Presently, she fell into step with several other members of staff as they walked along the corridor to Jasper's room, the door of which was already wide open. He was standing behind his desk, with Helen sitting alongside him, notebook and pen at the ready, and he greeted them all casually as they began sitting down on the two lines of chairs arranged in a semicircle in front of him.

From the place she'd chosen, right over to one side, Ria had deliberately placed herself out of his direct line of vision, but almost immediately she saw him glancing across at her and their eyes met for a fraction of a second—a second that seemed to linger for much longer than necessary as those intensely thoughtful eyes held her captive. And, despite all her best intentions, Ria felt a tremor of excitement sweep through her, making all her nerve-endings tingle, and she swallowed nervously. This was the first time she'd been anywhere close to her employer since the day she'd arrived, and even in this crowded room she felt again the leap of her pulse as her eyes flickered over him. He was sharp-suited as usual, the strong hair falling slightly over the expansive forehead, the uncompromising mouth set in a firm line. But it was his persona, the definable presence of the man which gripped her, and it was not what she wanted The last thing in the world that she wanted was being emotionally seduced—again—by another self-assertive alpha male. She was in unlooked for, dangerous waters and she bit her lip. She hoped that if she was asked to contribute to the meeting she'd be able to find her voice and say something sensible.

It proved to be a routine affair and at seven o'clock Jasper concluded the meeting. Ria stood up, relieved that nothing had been asked of her. But then, suddenly, he called across and she turned to look back at him.

'Ria, would you mind staying for a few moments, please?' he said—and it was not exactly a request.

She paused uncertainly, fiddling with the clasp of her bag and wondering why she was being singled out. Presently, after the chairs had been stacked neatly away again and everyone else had left, he gestured for her to come and sit opposite him once more.

'Now,' he said, looking directly at her, 'I want to know how everything's going for you. I didn't think for a minute that you'd want to air any problems in public. So fire away.'

Although his expression was serious, the voice was warm enough and Ria felt herself relaxing. She smiled, shrugging slightly.

'Well, actually, so far there haven't been any problems— none that I'm aware of,' she added. 'Lessons have been un-complicated, and I think I've got their interest—most of the time.' She smiled again. 'I haven't had to wake anyone up so far, anyway.'

He nodded slowly, remembering the other time she'd sat in that chair and how wonderful she'd looked then. And today was no exception, he acknowledged, her black narrow-leg trousers and crisp white shirt giving her a brisk, efficient air. And her glorious hair, just slightly out of place today, with a few fronds escaping to fall towards the curve of her cheeks only added to her appeal. He picked up a pen, trying not to keep looking at her.

'Tim has already told me that he's never known class three to be so well-behaved, or to show such concentration.' He paused for a moment, remembering Tim's enthusiastic opinion about Ria. ' So…' he looked up and smiled, his teeth white against his tanned skin '…well done,' he murmured. 'You seem to have fitted in very well—as I anticipated,' he added.

Ria was genuinely thrilled to be told that. She couldn't remember anyone bothering to compliment her on her work before, and it was true that she'd felt a special empathy with the class she'd been entrusted with.

'Well, thank you,' she said simply. 'I'm enjoying teaching these children more than any I've come across so far. I hope I can keep it up,' she added.

There was silence for a few moments, then, 'Actually, there is a small point which is bothering me…' she said slowly, and

Jasper raised his eyebrows. 'It concerns Josh…' she began, and he interrupted.

'Joshua Mills? Our new boy?'

Ria hesitated before going on. She didn't want to make a minor problem worse by saying too much about it. 'I think he's rather…unhappy…at the moment,' she said.

Jasper nodded. 'I'm not really surprised,' he said. 'Of course, it's very unusual for us to take any new student at this point of the year, but his parents are having severe personal problems at the moment, which are apparently not helped by their son being at home and getting under their feet. Joshua was not due here until September,' he added.

Suddenly the rugged features were dark with distaste as he went on. 'In my view, vulnerable children are not things, to be put in convenient boxes at given times.' He paused and leaned back in his chair. 'But, after thinking long and hard about it, I decided that being here was perhaps the kindest option for him—and Matron and his House Mistress are well aware of his particular problem.'

'Well, that probably does explain quite a lot,' Ria said. She paused. 'And it doesn't help that he is so much smaller than the rest of his year.' She didn't want to confess that seeing Josh, with his brown eyes looking at her pensively through rather large thick-framed spectacles, had made her want to gather him up in her arms.

'None of the others have been getting at him, have they?' Jasper said suddenly. 'No bullying, I hope?'

'Not that I've seen,' Ria said, hesitating for a moment before going on. 'Though there *is* something that's really bothering him.' She paused. 'It's about the tennis tournament.'

'What about it?'

'A couple of boys have told him that anyone refusing to take part will be severely punished.'

'Rubbish,' Jasper said flatly. 'It's certainly true that we encourage everyone to participate because it creates team spirit, with House against House, and as a school we believe that competition exposes talent and breeds excellence.' His mouth twisted slightly as he recalled the battles, masquerading as games of tennis, which he and Carl had fought in their youth, matching each other, shot for shot, each deadly serious and determined to win. He glanced across at Ria. 'But punishing those who really do not want to take part is a fiction,' he said.

Ria was relieved. 'I didn't believe it,' she said, 'but Josh does. So I'll be able to put his mind at rest about that, at least.'

Jasper looked across at her thoughtfully. 'You've obviously gained his confidence very quickly, Ria,' he said.

'Well, he does stay behind for a few moments after class, and we have a little chat,' Ria admitted. 'He told me that he's never enjoyed anything to do with sport—to the annoyance and regret of his father, apparently.'

Jasper tilted his head to one side briefly. 'Joshua is certainly a very academic child,' he said. 'His grasp of mathematics is awesome, I believe—so he probably prefers to grapple with complex theorems rather than hitting balls over nets, or anywhere else, for that matter.'

'He told me he was often expected to play tennis for hours on end, and hated every minute of it,' Ria went on. 'Couldn't see the point of it at all. Consequently, he was always rubbish at it—his words.' She smiled, pausing. 'The thing is—he's afraid of looking a wimp in front of all the others when he misses the shots all the time or, worse, if he asks to be given dispensation.'

Jasper's eyes narrowed thoughtfully, then, after a moment, 'Um…well…I think we can fix that easily enough,' he said. He leaned forward to scribble something down on the pad in front of him. 'Joshua can be one of the umpires,' he said. 'At least in the early heats. He obviously knows the game through and through, so there'll be no question of him getting the scoring wrong.' He smiled suddenly. 'It'll make him feel very superior to be sitting up there above everyone else—a job usually given to the older students, but that's not an unbreakable rule. Joshua can take his turn at doing the honours as well this time.'

What a clever headmaster! Ria thought. She'd been almost as worried as the child about the problem, but Jasper Trent had seen his way through it straight away. It was the perfect answer, and she knew Josh would be relieved.

'That's a wonderful idea, Jasper,' she said, her eyes bright with pleasure. She'd been half-expecting him to say that most of us would like to get out of things from time to time and that facing our demons was a necessary character-building exercise. But he'd sorted out Josh's problem in a flash—and Ria could have hugged him for it.

'As a matter of fact,' she went on, 'I empathized immediately with what Josh was going through as soon as he told me about it because I had a similar anxiety myself—and one which has never really gone away,' she added slowly.

'About…tennis?' Jasper asked curiously.

'No, no, my phobia was swimming. Deep water, in fact,' Ria admitted, looking away thoughtfully for a second. 'I suppose my long years in boarding schools have been reasonably happy—generally speaking,' she went on guardedly, 'but at one particular place I was singled out in swimming lessons as a total coward because I dreaded the annual gala. I was terrified that I was going to drown, and everyone, absolutely everyone, was forced to take part, and one sports mistress thought the way to cure me of my fears was to keep picking on me and making me do what I really hated—which was to completely immerse myself in order to pick up a brick lying on the bottom of the pool.' Ria shuddered at the memory. 'I became almost paralysed with fear every time the water closed over my head, when I wasn't able to breathe or see anything, and the sound of the water rushing in my ears haunts me in my dreams to this day.' She smiled quickly, realizing that she had never confided this to anyone else since. 'I was always sick for days before the event,' she admitted, 'and had nightmares after it.' She gave a short laugh and shrugged. 'But, despite my worst fears, I have lived to tell the tale—as you see.'

Jasper's face had become more and more sober at her words. 'Didn't you tell someone else how you felt?' he asked. 'Surely your parents should have known about it.'

'Oh, well, I never saw my parents for long enough at any one time to go into discussions about anything like that. Anyway,' Ria went on casually, 'it was the time when my mother walked out of the marriage, and my father had slightly more pressing worries than silly hang-ups which his only child might be having.'

Jasper's reaction to what she'd been saying was etched on his handsome features as he listened, and his dark brows knitted slightly. He cleared his throat. 'So—it's obviously put you off swimming for life?' he asked, and Ria shook her head.

'To my great surprise, I do swim—actually, quite well,' she said slowly. 'But I simply cannot dive. I cannot bring myself to go head first into deep water. It would feel like committing myself to hell—and I just know that I will never, ever forget that feeling of desperate panic. Pathetic, isn't it?'

'I don't think that's pathetic,' he said slowly. 'What I do think pathetic is the behaviour of an unimaginative teacher who couldn't find another way of handling your situation. Her answer to the problem was bullying you—and that should have been an unacceptable answer.'

By now, it was getting quite late and Jasper looked at his

watch suddenly. 'Oh, dear—dinner must be well under way,' he said. 'Sorry to have kept you, Ria.' He stood up, and Ria stood as well.

'Actually, I didn't order any dinner for tonight,' she said. 'As I wasn't sure what time the meeting would end…and I do have some work to finish.'

'I'm not going down, either,' he said, 'because I was obliged to attend a business lunch today, so all I need now is a drink.'

Ria followed him as he moved across to open the door for her. Although he was powerfully built, she thought briefly, it was his muscular strength, not excess body weight, which was apparent. All to do with regular workouts in a gym somewhere, she imagined.

Back in her flat, Ria threw her bag down on the bed and went across to the small kitchen. She, too, had eaten at lunch time, having found the time to make herself an omelette. But that was a long time ago and now she was feeling distinctly hungry.

She suddenly remembered the bottle of dry white wine which Hannah had given her as a present and, taking down one of the only two wine glasses she possessed, she poured herself a generous amount and too a large sip. She seldom drank when she was by herself, but tonight something had made her feel the need of it and at once she felt the liquid make her throat tingle pleasantly.

Suddenly, she spotted a couple of packages on top of her fridge, and she smiled. The housekeeper—a slight middle-aged woman with seemingly boundless energy—ran the domestic side of things with good-natured efficiency, looking after the staff like a mother, and Ria often found small, unexpected treats left for her to add to her cupboard. This time it was a soft, still slightly warm loaf of brown bread, and in the other bag were two perfect ripe peaches. Ria's mouth watered. What more did anyone need? Especially as yesterday she'd bought a small piece of local cheese and four tomatoes from the farm shop situated a few hundred yards from the school entrance. Tonight's menu would be the perfect answer to her hunger pangs, she thought.

But first she felt the need to undress and relax. Getting out of her work clothes always made her feel that the busy day had really come to an end and that it was time to switch off. And she admitted that although all her lessons, so far, had gone well—on the whole—she sometimes felt an undeniable tide of stress sweep over her. But being here alone in her little flat was the perfect antidote.

She went into the bathroom and slipped out of her clothes, suddenly deciding to wash her hair now, rather than leave it until the morning. And, since there was plenty of time before bed, it could dry naturally, she decided. She could always finish off later with the hairdryer.

Presently, she shrugged into her favourite cream cotton dressing gown and started to towel her hair briskly, padding barefoot out of the bathroom as she went. Suddenly, two short taps on her door made her stop in her tracks, and she paused. Oh, no, she thought, she didn't want visitors tonight, thank you very much. Sighing, she went across to see who was there.

It was Jasper, and she almost froze to the spot as she looked up at him. How *embarrassing* to be caught out in this state! Then she felt cross. After all, she was perfectly entitled to be in whatever state she liked at this time of the day. She smiled, trying to appear unconcerned.

There was a short silence. Then—'Sorry to disturb you, Ria,' he said casually, 'but I completely forgot to give you this earlier. Tim asked me to let you have it before tomorrow morning—he wasn't at the meeting, as you know, because he's on House duty this evening.'

He gazed down at her. The flimsy dressing gown she had

on did nothing to disguise the tempting body beneath, and the huge white towel wrapped around her head like a turban succeeded in emphasizing the lustre of her widely spaced eyes. She was getting to him—again—he thought, and he cleared his throat unnecessarily.

'I'm sorry that I've clearly come at a very inconvenient moment,' he said, 'but I just need to point out a couple of things on this…' He indicated some papers in his hand.

Ria stepped aside, suddenly not caring about her present state. Well, so what? she thought. It was his own fault, not hers, that he'd found her like this, and it certainly hadn't appeared to faze him. He just stood there, one eyebrow raised quizzically. She shrugged inwardly, suddenly feeling devil-may-care and upbeat—thanks, no doubt, to that glass of good wine, she thought.

'Please do come in,' she said.

He grinned, and came in at once, closing the door behind him.

'This'll only take a few seconds,' he said, following her inside. 'It's a slight change of plan for first period tomorrow.'

Without waiting to be asked, he sat down on one of the chairs by the small table and Ria sat opposite him and for the next few minutes Jasper pointed out the directions which Tim had asked him to make clear.

Suddenly, as Ria leaned forward to scrutinize the details on the sheet, the towel around her head disentangled itself and fell on to the table in front of them and her wet hair cascaded down around her, covering her face for a second.

'Oh—*sorry*,' she gasped, grabbing the towel with one hand and pulling her hair away with the other. Looking down quickly, she saw that the ink on the papers had already smudged some of Tim's alterations and she gazed across helplessly. 'Sorry about that,' she repeated.

Suddenly they both laughed, and for the first time since

she'd come to Highbridge Manor Ria felt that a sea change had happened between her and her employer. She accepted that it always took her quite a time to settle in to a new situation, to know where she stood with colleagues or superiors, and so far she hadn't felt entirely easy about Jasper Trent—not that she'd seen that much of him yet. However pleasant he appeared, she couldn't help feeling that he was constantly making mental notes about her—and from a very safe and superior distance. And the dark, enigmatic glances he gave her now and then only made it worse. Whatever went on in that handsome head was his own, very well-kept, secret.

'I'd better sort myself out for a moment,' she said, getting up quickly and going into her bathroom.

Fortunately, much of the excess water had gone from her hair now, and Ria was able to brush the tangled waves out in long strokes to make it look more presentable. But she sighed briefly as she glanced in the mirror at her shiny nose and face—every scrap of make-up had been thoroughly washed away, she realized. Then she shrugged. Did she really care what she looked like in front of Jasper Trent? Don't answer that, she told herself.

He was still sitting there when she went back in again, and she wondered if he'd said everything he had to say. Then she remembered something she'd meant to ask Tim—and, since the headmaster was here, she might as well ask him instead. She sat down again opposite him.

'Jasper, I've been thinking—would there be any objection if I included some poetry appreciation in the timetable?' she asked. 'I know it's not part of the present curriculum—which, of course, I'll complete—but I think there'd be time to fit in some poetry as well.' She paused, hoping she wasn't putting her foot in it. 'The thing is, during some discussion at the end of lessons the other day I got the impression that the boys would appreciate it—well, some of them would.' She paused. 'It is something I feel on very safe ground with,' she added earnestly.

He barely hesitated before replying. 'Feel free,' he said. 'Just let Tim know what you intend doing.' His eyes had not left her as she'd been speaking. She looked ridiculously child-like in her bedtime attire, he thought, acknowledging a rush of desire to get closer to her as the folds of her dressing gown slipped apart slightly at the front, exposing a firm thigh and slim leg for a brief second…

Sensing something new in the atmosphere, Ria took this totally bizarre situation into her own hands. It was time for her boss to go.

'Look,' she said, 'I'm suddenly desperate for my supper…' She paused awkwardly. 'Um…would you like to share some fresh bread and cheese?' she asked, knowing that he'd take the hint and refuse.

But he didn't refuse, and it almost made Ria fall off her chair when he said unexpectedly, 'Thanks—why not?'

After she'd got over her amazement, it only took a few moments for Ria to put the simple meal out on the table, and she smiled briefly as she looked across at him. 'I'm afraid all I can offer you is a glass of white wine,' she said. 'No whisky or other spirits…'

He was standing over by the window, and he turned to look at her. 'Just a coffee would be fine, thanks,' he said. 'I'll put the kettle on,' he added, going over to fill it under the tap.

When they'd eaten the slices of bread, and almost finished off two of the tomatoes and the portion of cheese between them, Ria took the peaches and stoned and sliced them deftly, arranging one on a plate and handing it over to Jasper. 'We've got Claudia to thank for these,' she said, putting one of the slices into her mouth, and cupping her hand under her chin to catch the juice before it dribbled down. 'She's always spoiling me. I never know what will turn up next.'

Jasper gazed at her moist lips, feeling his own mouth water. He raised his eyes. 'Well, she doesn't leave anything for me—unless I specifically ask her to,' he said. 'You're obviously one of her favourites, Ria. You must tell me your secret.'

Almost an hour had elapsed since he'd turned up so un-expectedly, and Ria realized—with a huge degree of sur-prise—just how quickly the time had gone. They suddenly seemed like two friends—two people who'd known each other for ages—she thought as they sipped the last of the coffee.

Presently, just as he stood up to leave, Ria's mobile rang and she frowned. It was rather late for a call from Sara or Hannah—or from anyone wanting a chat, she thought, going into her bedroom to answer it. As she clicked it on she was confused at first to hear her father's voice. It was several months since he'd rung her.

'Dad?' she said uncertainly. 'Is anything wrong?'

'Nothing's wrong at all, Ria,' he said. 'It's just that Diana and I are going to be in Taunton tomorrow. I've a meeting in the morning, and we were wondering whether you could join us for dinner later on. I've forgotten where you are at the moment—you're not still in the London area, are you? I think you said that the job there had come to an end. I have a vague recollection of you saying that you were going to stay with a friend in Salisbury for a while…and, if that's the case, it wouldn't be too difficult for you to meet up with us at Taunton, would it?'

'No—no, I'm sure it wouldn't be,' Ria said quickly. It was so good to hear his voice after the considerable length of time which had elapsed since they'd spoken.

'And I could probably manage that,' she went on, 'as I'm teaching at a school in Hampshire at the moment. I don't finish lessons until four-thirty to five, though, so it would have to be a bit later on before I could get to Taunton…'

'Oh, that doesn't matter,' her father said at once. 'We're staying over and I'm sure there will be something to eat.' There was a pause. 'It would be great to see you again, Ria, and to catch up with all your news. Especially as I'm afraid we're off abroad again at the weekend and I'm not sure when we'll be back,' he said. 'And Diana was insistent that I got in touch so that we could meet up. She's longing to see you again,' he added.

A mental picture of her stepmother filled Ria's thoughts—the lovely Diana, blonde-haired and beautiful and almost half her father's age. And, although Diana and Ria hadn't had that much opportunity to be together, they had got on well from the start.

'It's going to be great to see you both,' Ria said. 'And I'm sure I can find the hotel. Shall we say somewhere between eight o'clock and eight-thirty?'

They ended the call and Ria went back to see Jasper at the sink rinsing their modest amount of washing-up. She stood watching him for a second, and he glanced at her quickly.

'Something wrong?' he asked casually, folding the tea towel he'd been using and putting it back in its place.

'No, nothing's wrong,' Ria replied lightly. 'That was my father.' She paused. 'We haven't spoken for a long time and he wants me to go to Taunton tomorrow evening and meet him—and my stepmother—for dinner. I told him I couldn't get there until later anyway, but since they're only in the UK until the weekend I mustn't pass up this chance, must I?' She started to put the dishes away. 'I've never actually been to Taunton,' she said as an afterthought, 'but I'm sure I'll be able to find it.'

Jasper went across to the door and looked back at her. 'Well, your luck's in,' he said briefly. 'Because I'm going back home to my place tomorrow, which isn't a million miles away from Taunton. I could drop you off first, wherever you're meeting, and pick you up again later on—probably about midnight. Will that do?'

Ria felt a rush of relief—she hated finding new places, especially if countless roundabouts and one-way systems were involved, as they undoubtedly would be.

'Oh—brilliant!' she said. 'If you're sure that taking me wouldn't be mucking up your own plans,' she added.

'Well, I volunteered,' he reminded her easily.

He wasn't going to tell her that he'd actually intended staying the night at the cottage and not coming back until later on Friday. But somehow he felt that it was very important for Ria to see her family—to Jasper, their relationship seemed to need a little care and attention. And, in adjusting his own plans, he was only doing his headmasterly duty in making life as easy as possible for a member of his staff, he told himself.

CHAPTER FIVE

THE following evening, Ria looked fondly across at her father as he leaned back in his chair at the table, twirling the brandy around in his glass contentedly. He had always been a very good-looking man and he was wearing his age well, she admitted, with barely a trace of grey in his dark hair and a figure showing no sign of paunchiness. And the glances he constantly gave his wife told their own story—they were a couple who were very much in love and didn't mind letting everyone know it. And tonight Diana was looking extremely fetching. She was wearing a simple white, almost off-the-shoulder dress, her naturally blonde hair—much longer than Ria remembered it—drifting in natural waves at her neckline. Her only jewellery seemed to be the expensive diamond solitaire nestling against the wide gold wedding band on her finger.

They had all enjoyed the excellent meal—and the easy conversation which had accompanied it—and Ria felt rather wistful that their chances to be together were so few. They'd been speaking mostly about her own career, and especially about Highbridge Manor, and of her father's commitments abroad, with Diana hanging on his every word.

Suddenly, Ria said, 'You never minded giving up your own profession, Diana? In order to accompany my father around the globe?' Before her marriage Diana had been a much sought-after psychiatric therapist attached to a leading teaching hospital.

Diana smiled quickly at the thought. 'Never for a single moment, Ria,' she said. 'I'm enjoying every moment of my life.'

Just then a waiter appeared with a large bottle of the best champagne in an ice bucket and Ria looked up, surprised. They had already enjoyed some very good wine with their meal. But the reason for it was soon made clear as her father leaned forward to give the two women their brim-full glasses.

'We've been wondering which one of us should actually tell you our great news, Ria,' he said, 'and in the end Diana proposed that it should be me.' He looked across and held Diana's gaze for a second, and as she saw their eyes meet intimately Ria's heart fluttered uncomfortably. 'I hope it won't be too much of a shock for you,' he went on, 'but—we are absolutely thrilled to tell you that my wife expects to make me a very proud father before the end of the year.'

At about eleven-thirty, in the hotel's Ladies room, Ria stood with her forehead placed against the ornate mirror on the wall, trying to regain control of her emotions. She knew that if she took long, measured breaths she could calm the heightened beating of her heart to something approaching normality. She stood away and stared at the face looking back at her, at the huge eyes moist with unshed tears, and shook her head briefly. Would she feel normal, really normal, ever again? she asked herself.

She had managed to respond very enthusiastically to the news of the forthcoming happy event, hugging Diana to her tightly. 'That's fantastic, Diana,' she'd said. 'Congratulations!' And of course it was fantastic...but, because it was something Ria had never contemplated, never given a thought to, it had been a shock. A physical shock.

She decided to call Jasper on his mobile—they'd exchanged numbers in case of any emergency or change of plan, and a small wave of pleasure ran through her as she heard his voice.

'Hi, there,' he said at once. 'To what do I owe the pleasure?'

'It's just that I'm actually ready to leave now,' Ria said, 'and I wondered whether it would be convenient for you to pick me up sooner than we agreed.'

'It would be entirely convenient,' he replied, 'as I'm sitting in a pub just up the road.' There was a pause. 'Will two minutes do?'

'It will do very well, thank you,' Ria replied, and something in her tone of voice made Jasper frown briefly. He hoped the reunion had gone as planned. 'I'll wait outside the hotel entrance,' Ria added briefly before finishing the call.

She returned to the lounge and sat down to rejoin the others. 'My lift has just rung to ask if he can pick me up a bit early,' she lied, 'so—I'll have to love you and leave you, I'm afraid.' She smiled brightly. 'It's been…great…to see you again.'

'Yes, it's been lovely,' her stepmother agreed, 'and we mustn't leave it so long next time, Ria, must we? After all, I shall be expecting some support from a certain favourite relative!' Diana glanced across at her husband. 'I'm also hoping that one day in the not too distant future—especially now—Mark might be based a bit nearer home,' she added.

Ria's father smiled gently and took his wife's hand. 'I did warn you what to expect, sweetheart,' he said. 'But times they are a-changing! So, who knows?'

They insisted on coming outside to wait with her for Jasper. Ria hoped that when he arrived he would just pull up, let her get in and drive off again. But, as it happened, he had already parked slightly out of their sight and almost at once his tall figure could be seen striding towards them.

'Oh, Jasper—this is my father, and my stepmother, Diana,'

she began and, looking up at her father, she said, 'and this is Jasper Trent, Dad—the Head of the school I've been telling you all about. My present employer,' she added, as if that needed saying.

As they murmured their gracious individual greetings, Jasper took in the situation at a glance. Ria certainly had a very attractive, socially adept family, he acknowledged, but it was patently obvious to him, even at this brief meeting, that something wasn't quite right. And Ria, in her long, flowing, patterned ethnic-type skirt and flimsy top, her hair pulled back in a long ponytail, to him looked somehow painfully defenceless. Of course, he was already aware of her background, but there seemed more to it than that. Whatever it was that hung so notably in the air made Jasper want to take her in his arms and bundle her into the car. To get her out of here—to get her away.

And within a few minutes he did just that, with the others standing at the entrance of the hotel, waving them out of sight.

As he accelerated away, Jasper glanced across at Ria briefly. He didn't need telling that seeing her family again had been a mixed blessing. Her hands were clasped tightly together in her lap, her expression—even in the restricted light—seemed troubled.

He cleared his throat. 'So…have you had a good evening?' he asked casually, keeping his eyes on the road.

Ria paused before replying. 'It was rather a…long…evening.' She paused. 'A great deal seems to be happening for them all the time. They seem to have a very full diary,' she added quietly.

She looked away. She didn't want to talk about it—not to Jasper, anyway. Hannah was the only friend to whom she could pour out her heart, because it was only Hannah who knew everything about her, who understood. As Ria's thoughts ran on, Seth's handsome face came into her mind. Where was he now? she wondered aimlessly, then made a face to herself. Wherever he was, she knew he would be enjoying his life to the full. That was a given. He had never let anything stand in the way of his determination to do that, and he'd be making sure that no tiresome shackles hindered him or held him back. And he'd always seemed to get away with it, she remembered.

'So…what did they think of your plans to travel?' Jasper asked, bringing Ria back to the present with a jolt.

'Oh—I actually forgot to mention that,' Ria said casually. 'There seemed to be many more interesting things for us to talk about.'

Jasper raised his eyebrows but said no more, and they travelled in silence for a few minutes, Jasper's mind flicking back to his impressions of Ria's family. He had to admit that her stepmother was an extremely pretty woman—something of a trophy wife for her husband, he thought wryly—but no competition for Ria. In his opinion, Ria possessed that something, that indefinable characteristic given to very few—the ability to captivate any male—anyone—who crossed her path, without even trying.

Presently, whatever her feelings, Ria knew that she must at least try to make pleasant conversation. Jasper had been good enough to bring her this evening—which she was hugely grateful to him for. If she'd had to drive herself back now, she honestly wondered if she'd be capable of it, because all she felt like doing was curling up in a dark corner somewhere.

She looked across at him now and smiled briefly. 'What about your own arrangements—were you able to do what you'd planned?' she asked. He had already told her that there were certain things to be sorted at his cottage.

'Oh—yes, thanks,' he said. 'I just had to give my approval

for some new furnishings we've been considering before we ordered them, that's all.'

So, Ria thought, there *was* a woman in his life—probably not a wife, but a live-in lover who was obviously not trusted to make important decisions by herself. But then, Ria could well imagine that Jasper's opinion would have to be paramount in all things.

For some reason, what he had just said made Ria feel more downbeat than ever—not about the fact that Jasper Trent and his lady-love were selecting new additions to their home, but that he was not single, after all. And why did that thought affect *her*—even remotely? But of course it didn't, she assured herself. Not one bit. She was just feeling miserable at the moment, that was all—and she bit her lips hard to try and stop them from trembling. Meeting up with her family tonight hadn't done her many favours after all, she thought.

Somehow, she managed to drag herself away from her mental turmoil and think of things to say and, glancing across at him, she saw that the scar on his cheek seemed slightly more noticeable tonight. Without even thinking, and with unusual impulsiveness, she put her hand up and traced it gently with her finger.

'How did that happen, Jasper?' she asked, and at her touch his body stiffened, the designer jeans he was wearing suddenly seeming a couple of sizes too small. He looked back at her quickly.

'Oh—that was a long time ago, back in my Cambridge days,' he said. 'A very unfriendly rugby boot caught me unawares—but we won the game,' he added, smiling briefly.

Ria clasped her hands together again, conscious of how her pulse had quickened as she'd stroked his face for that fleeting second or two, how firm and desirable his skin had felt beneath her fingertips. How her breasts had tingled with that half-forgotten sensitivity… Swallowing hard, and with a sense of desperation, she took control of herself again.

'I've hardly seen anything of Helen,' she remarked, saying the first thing that came into her head. 'Not since the first evening, really.'

'No, she's always extremely busy—and her mother isn't well at the moment,' he replied at once. He glanced across, knowing that he was in dangerous waters when he was in too-close proximity to Ria Davidson. Of course he would always admire attractive females, and enjoy being in their company— that would never change—but looking at a woman and wanting to touch her, to feel her soft skin yield to the warm caress of his hands, were two different things. And, for the foreseeable future, certainly not part of his game plan, he told himself.

After that, their conversation almost immediately became centred on matters to do with the school, and the powerful car soon swallowed up the miles as they covered the distance.

But Jasper knew that, for Ria, the evening had not been entirely successful. His perceptiveness had picked up the vibes loud and clear. And, for a moment or two, he felt irritated with her. Of course he knew that she did not have a particularly happy family background—but that was the case for countless other people, other children. If ever he had any of his own—which was a highly unlikely prospect, he thought, they would always come first and be loved unconditionally. They would never be ignored or pushed from pillar to post. Or left to be brought up by others.

But Ria Davidson's own situation was not exactly dire, he thought. She had so much going for her. She'd had a sound education and was highly intelligent…and she was beautiful into the bargain. Surely a big plus for any woman—she had that much to thank her parents for. She was undoubtedly one of nature's favourites by any standards. Perhaps she should start to count her blessings and not keep old resentments intruding on her happiness. Suddenly, he felt like shaking her.

But that was until he glanced across at her again and felt himself melting. What he *really* wanted to do was to take her in his arms. To feel the feminine contours of her body meld with his own more muscular ones. He cursed inwardly. What the hell was the matter with him? Where were all his good intentions? But then he allowed himself a brief smile which tilted the corners of his mouth for a second. At least the woman's very temporary interruption to his life had proved one—rather important—point, he thought. He was not as emotionally paralysed as he'd begun to think, and that realization gave him a quiet moment of satisfaction. Because his one experience of totally trusting a woman with his life had convinced him that he'd never, ever be caught out again. Felicity had been his one big mistake, and it would never be repeated. It had been a steep learning curve, and it still hurt.

He leaned forward suddenly and fiddled pointlessly with something on the instrument panel. Despite the undeniable fact that she couldn't be faulted in the job he was paying her for, and had so far acted in exactly the appropriate way with his impressionable pupils, he needed Ria out of his life—soon, he told himself.

But, before that could happen, he had to survive seeing her for almost two more months. And somehow manage to keep a clear head.

It was very late when they arrived back at the school, and presently the two made their way quietly along to the side door to which all staff members had keys in order to gain access after the place had been locked up for the night.

Ria looked up at him as he selected his own key from the bunch in his hand. 'I'm really grateful to you for tonight,

Jasper,' she said. 'I'd have had real problems finding my own way across country once I'd left the motorway.' She paused. 'Besides which, your car is so much comfier than mine. And faster,' she added.

He paused, returning her glance. 'Well, I've made that journey many times—as you'd imagine,' he said, 'and every time it seems to get quicker. Anyway,' he added, 'I was happy to make it easy for you, Ria.'

They entered the building and walked up the stairs towards the flats, Ria stifling a yawn.

'Oh, dear,' she whispered. 'I'm beginning to feel really tired.'

'Hardly surprising,' he said mildly. 'You've done a day's teaching, after all, not to mention spending several hours nattering with your family. And travelling, however you do it, is always tiring. You'll probably go out like a light as soon as your head touches the pillow,' he added.

But she wasn't tired at all, Ria thought. All she wanted to do now was to get inside her room and be alone.

But she congratulated herself that she'd been able, after all, to sound reasonably normal with Jasper when they'd been in the car, had somehow succeeded in choking back her anguish. Hadn't started blubbing and blurting out things she'd be sorry for afterwards. Because he was the kind of man you *could* tell things to, she thought, if you weren't careful. The kind of man whom you could confide in, and who would never betray a confidence. Not that she'd ever, ever be sharing a certain part of her past with him. Somehow, she didn't think he'd understand.

As they approached her flat, Ria fumbled for the key—which always seemed to find its way to the very bottom corner of her bag, out of sight and, as Jasper stood patiently waiting for her to find it, she said, keeping her voice down, 'I was thinking, you must be very confident about the staff you employ at your firm, Jasper.' He had told her about the company he owned near Bath, making medical equipment. 'I mean—you seem so committed here, in every way. Is it difficult, wearing two hats?' she asked.

'Not really,' he said. 'I'm only a text or phone call away from the factory—and, in any case, I frequently put in an appearance there. Besides which, in any capacity, I always make a point of only employing first-rate people who can hold the fort and who can be trusted,' he added, smiling down at her darkly—but reminding himself that the one exception to the rule had been Ria's predecessor.

Where on earth was that wretched key? Ria thought, still fumbling for it. 'But will you be glad to be back full-time?' she persisted, at last feeling her fingers make contact with what she was looking for.

He nodded his head briefly to one side. 'Of course, it will obviously be more convenient,' he said, 'but I'll probably miss the boys, the rough and tumble of school life; that's inevitable.' He paused, slightly surprised at the admission. 'But you can't have everything, I suppose.'

They made their goodnights and, a moment or two later, and safely in her own room at last, Ria threw her bag down on the bed and stood quite still, feeling that she was in a vacuum—of utter pointlessness. Then, unable to stop it, a long uninterrupted wail left her throat as she sank to her knees on the floor and buried her face in her hands. This was her punishment—retribution for what she had done in her life— and there was no one to blame but herself.

And a mere few paces away, the plaintive, distinctive cry of a wounded animal reached Jasper's ears, a cry followed by stifled, heart-rending sobs.

Automatically, he stopped in his tracks and gritted his teeth. What the *hell* was going on? What was the matter with the woman? Turning, he strode back and rapped firmly on her door.

'Ria! Open the door!' he demanded.

Almost at once the sobbing became less audible as Ria gained control of herself and, in a few moments, she unlocked her door for him to come in. But she turned away, not looking at him as she went slowly into her bedroom, her shoulders hunched as she continued trying to wipe away her tears.

He followed her, staring down at her as she sat on the edge of her bed. After a moment he said quietly, 'Are you going to tell me what this is all about, Ria?'

Ria shook her head slowly. 'I...I could never make you understand...' she whispered.

'Try me,' he said flatly.

There was a long, long pause as Ria tried to find the words—words that might make sense to someone like Jasper Trent. Then she took a deep breath and looked up at him.

'It's just that...the real reason for all the champagne we drank this evening was that my stepmother is expecting a baby,' she said. 'On Christmas Day or thereabouts I'm going to be presented with a half-brother or -sister.'

Jasper was clearly mystified as to why this fact should be causing Ria so much grief. 'So...then...isn't that wonderful news?' he asked quietly. 'Aren't you pleased for them?'

Well, of course he would take that attitude, Ria thought helplessly. Why shouldn't he? But this was hardly a good moment to tell him—or anyone—that, if things had been different, *she* should be the proud mother of a beautiful child, that by this time her own baby should have been taking its first steps, should have been smiling back at her as she rocked it in her arms.

'Of course I'm pleased for them,' she said slowly, 'and it's difficult to put into words why the news came as such a shock.' She attempted a watery smile. 'Perhaps I find it hard to imagine my father being a parent again—at his age,' she admitted. 'I honestly never gave it a thought, but of course I should have done. Diana is still a young woman… I obviously had my head well in the sand,' she added, tears starting to seep from her eyes again.

A glimmer of understanding flickered across Jasper's features as he listened to what Ria was saying and he shrugged inwardly. Although she probably didn't even realize it, Ria may be feeling slightly resentful that she was to share her father with a sibling after all this time, he thought. Especially as it was obvious that there had been a rather sad lack of attentiveness towards her all the time she'd been growing up.

Whatever the reason, the effect the present situation had on Jasper was to make him want to undress her and lie with her on the bed…to cover her body with his kisses and caresses…to possess her.

He bent slowly and took her hands in his, pulling her gently to her feet. 'It's been a long day, Ria… What can I do to help you? There *must* be something.' Because he knew he couldn't just leave her there by herself to grieve…for, whatever reason, she was so…so sad, he thought helplessly. Then, slowly and with a tiny shudder of release, of relief, she collapsed against him and he automatically, expertly, folded her into his arms, then tilted her head back gently and closed his mouth over her parted lips. To Ria, it was like a magical dream sequence and their kiss—their unbelievable kiss—was slow, moist and sensuous as she felt the hardening of his body, felt the strong thudding of his heart against her breasts, and she realized that she had never felt such overwhelming desire before in her life. Never, never. This was a once-in-a-life experience. For her, the whole evening had seemed surreal—and this unimaginable part of it was the most surreal of all. Surreal—and erotic.

Afterwards, she couldn't remember how long they had stayed there as she clung to him. How long she'd allowed him to claim and reclaim her lips, to kiss her neck and throat and her eyes—still wet with tears—until she had become calm at last.

And then, satisfied that he could safely leave her alone, he had released her and turned abruptly, leaving the room without another word.

And presently, spent and exhausted, Ria lay beneath her duvet, willing sleep to come—and bring with it spectacular dreams that would make every nerve in her body tingle with the hot desire she had experienced clasped there in Jasper Trent's arms.

CHAPTER SIX

WHEN she awoke the next morning, it was some time before Ria could bring herself to open her eyes. Everything that had happened yesterday was as clear as crystal as she went over and over it all in her mind, and it came as a profound shock to realize, in the cool light of day, just how readily she had surrendered to Jasper's claiming of her lips, and the sexual excitement she'd experienced. His raw masculinity had taken her completely by surprise, and she knew she had clung to him, the surging tide of warmth coursing through her veins making her limp and helpless in his arms. And when eventually he had released her, she could see her own amazement mirrored in his smouldering eyes.

Lying there, reliving those unforgettable moments, Ria suddenly froze as her thoughts ran on. Would what had happened between them last night affect her career at Highbridge Manor? she asked herself. How would Jasper view the situation—view *her* situation? Or maybe the incident, to him, would be just that—an incident—which he'd already forgotten.

Ria bit her lip. She wished she hadn't opened the door to him after they'd said their goodnights…wished that he hadn't come into her flat. Because she knew she was going to feel bad when they came to face to face.

Suddenly she threw off her duvet and sat up. She must try and put all of yesterday completely out of her mind and get life back into some sort of perspective, Ria told herself. When she'd been told about Diana's forthcoming baby, she had succeeded in sharing in their joy and excitement—and she *was* pleased for them; she really was. But it would be hard to confess to anyone why their news had come as such a painful shock to her.

Going into the bathroom, she reached for her toothbrush and started cleaning her teeth vigorously, then stopped for a second as she suddenly remembered something exquisite just beginning to surface in her mind…because, in her haunted dreams, she'd lifted her hand and traced that scar on Jasper's cheek again, and he had kissed her fingers slowly, gently, taking his time, before putting them into his mouth, one by one. And, even now, as she was desperately trying to put her thoughts into some sort of order, she could feel the delicious movement of his tongue against her flesh. Hurriedly, she began scrubbing her teeth again—this would not do, she told herself. It simply would not do.

Presently, after she'd showered and got dressed, she went across to the window and drew back the curtains. In the near distance she could see that the boarders were already up and about, one or two kicking a ball around on the small patch of ground immediately in front of their quarters, while others stood leaning against the wall, chatting, pushing each other, generally mucking about. Sighing, she realized that today was just another working day. Yesterday was history, and now her job must be her only thought.

Frowning suddenly, she remembered another small point which had temporarily eluded her—Jasper Trent was already spoken for, wasn't he? What had he been thinking of last night? For those few moments when he had held her close to him, he had certainly not been thinking of the woman back home in Somerset! And how could she, Ria, have allowed it to happen? Especially as she knew he'd regretted it almost as soon as it had taken place. That was obvious from the way he'd made such an abrupt and hasty retreat.

Turning away, Ria went into the kitchen area and put the kettle on. Breakfast was available for everyone from seven a.m.—but she had only ordered breakfast three times since her arrival, preferring to eat up here alone—and, anyway, tea and toast was as much as she could manage first thing.

At eight-twenty, wearing her fine grey tailored trousers and white T-shirt, and with her hair swept up as usual, Ria made her way to the main assembly hall. The boys were already sitting quietly in their places to await the arrival of the deputy head, who always led the daily ritual.

At precisely eight-thirty a bell rang somewhere outside and immediately everyone stood up. But today—and for the first time since Ria had been at the school—it was Jasper who strode down the centre aisle and stepped up onto the stage.

He was immaculately dressed as usual, his whole bearing demonstrating his authority, and, despite having given herself that strong talking-to earlier, Ria's heart leapt several paces as she gazed up at him. Why had fate been so cruel in letting *him* cross her path now, at this time of her life? she thought. She did not want her feelings, her emotions, her longings, stirred up ever again. To her dismay, she felt a wave of nausea sweep over her for a second.

And, having a bird's-eye view from his elevated position on the stage, Jasper had homed in on Ria straight away, and that muscle in his neck twitched briefly at the sight of her. He saw that she was quietly composed, her face wan, her expression listless and he almost melted as he looked at her. But what had happened between them last night had been unexpected—

and dramatic—and he'd been cursing himself for it ever since. Whatever must she think of him? he asked himself. He'd put her in an impossible position, barging into her room like that, demanding to know what was wrong. It was unforgivable of him. And where was his well-known assertion that he didn't believe in mixing business with pleasure? What had happened to that? Ria Davidson was a vulnerable member of his staff, and he knew he'd stepped right out of line. And even though he was only too aware that she had yielded willingly to his advances, the reason for that was clear enough. The news about her family had seemed to totally unsettle her, and what she'd needed just then had been some comfort and reassurance—and he'd given it to her. But he should not have gone to those lengths, he told himself. He'd not done either of them any favours.

Despite all his inner thoughts, the items on the day's agenda were discussed and dealt with promptly and after some minutes Jasper brought the assembly to a close. He walked swiftly back down through the hall again and, as he came alongside the row where Ria was standing, he glanced across at her as he went by.

'Could you spare me two minutes, please, Miss Davidson?' he said. Then he was gone, and everyone dispersed and went their separate ways.

At the doorway, Tim came up to Ria. 'Is everything OK, Ria?' he asked. 'Are you feeling all right?' He'd noticed how pale Ria was looking.

She smiled up at him quickly. 'I'm fine, thanks, Tim.' She paused. 'I had a late night yesterday, that's all.' She turned to go, then, 'Oh, by the way, I've been wanting to see you, Tim. Would you be happy for me to include some poetry appreciation in one or two lessons—after I've covered everything else, of course? A few of the boys in Class Four have expressed an interest,' she added.

Tim grinned down at her. 'I can see no rhyme or reason why not—ha ha,' he said. 'As a matter of fact, we haven't covered much poetry for a while—perhaps we should look at that next year.'

Ria felt pleased at his reaction—not that she'd be here then, she thought.

She got to Jasper's room. The door was open and he was standing by the window speaking on the telephone. As soon as he saw her, he beckoned for her to come in, and she did, closing the door behind her.

Presently, he finished the call and glanced across at her. 'Come and sit down a minute, Ria,' he said.

Ria knew that her heart was banging uncomfortably and that her cheeks had gone bright crimson—and how could that be helped? she thought. Seeing Jasper again after what had happened between them last night was not only embarrassing—it was torture.

She sat down on the very edge of the chair and looked up at him and, as she'd expected, he came straight to the point.

'I wish to apologize for my behaviour last night,' he said flatly. He paused, searching for the right words. 'It…it was because I hated to see you so distressed,' he went on, 'and that's the only explanation I can offer you.' He swallowed. 'But I promise you that it will never happen again and I hope you can forget the whole thing as soon as possible.'

He needn't have bothered to put such a fine point on it, Ria thought dully, his words forming ice-cold splinters in her heart. Because a part—a very small part of her—would have liked to think that he had kissed her because he found her desirable, that in that poignant moment in the silence of her room he had actually wanted to. But he was leaving her in no doubt about the true facts. It had been an unfortunate one-off as far as he was concerned—well, was she really surprised? And she could easily understand how much he was regretting it.

By now, Ria was gaining control of the situation, and of herself, and she nodded slowly, deliberately. 'Actually,' she said coolly, 'I haven't thought about it since, Jasper. So there's absolutely no need for you to concern yourself further.'

How could she lie so convincingly? she asked herself. And how could she—how *would* she ever—forget the feeling of his body wrapped around her, of his magnetic lips fusing with hers?

'But perhaps I should add my own apologies,' she went on formally, 'for causing a situation that quite obviously took us both unawares,' she said. 'The fact was I drank far too much champagne earlier, and alcohol always makes me weepy. And probably hearing all the family news and seeing how upbeat and excited my father and stepmother were made me just lose my grip on reality, that's all.'

She stood up now, squaring her shoulders. 'But I'm fine today,' she said cheerfully, hoping he'd believe her. 'Absolutely fine. Yesterday is all in the past, Jasper—gone and forgotten, and now I'm raring to go to my next lesson and concentrate on what I like doing best.'

Jasper continued staring across at her as she spoke and, in spite of everything he had said, the urge to take her in his arms was almost unbearable. He cleared his throat. 'I've been thinking…how would it be if…would you like some time off, Ria?' he said suddenly. 'Maybe to stay with your friend for a few days?'

'Why?' she asked sharply, her colour rising again. 'Is…is my work at fault?'

'Of course not,' he said. He paused. 'You've been here just over a month, and giving it your all, I know that. Tim is very pleased with everything you're doing—but maybe a few days away from school would do you good.' It would do him good, too, he thought, to put some distance between them until he really had gained control of his personal life again. He looked down at her soberly. 'Sometimes a bit of respite doesn't come amiss,' he added.

'No, thank you,' she said flatly. 'I don't need a rest—I'm feeling OK. I told you, I'm just a bit tired this morning, that's all.'

He nodded his head to one side. 'Well, it's up to you. The offer's there.' He couldn't tell her that he was aware that something pretty significant was going on in her mind, however much she was blaming everything on that champagne. And he'd thought that a few days with her friend in Salisbury might do her some good.

He shrugged. 'Anyway, it's Friday—which I know is always a busy one,' he said, 'but at least you'll have the weekend to rest up a bit.'

Ria stood up to go, feeling slightly awkward now. Was this a first step towards getting rid of her early, of terminating her contract? 'Well, anyway, thank you for your concern—' she faltered '—but I'm fine, absolutely fine,' she repeated, wishing with all her heart that that were true.

If she didn't get out now, Jasper thought, he'd do something he'd be sorry for—again. He followed her to the door, just as Helen arrived, clutching some files under her arm.

'Ah, Helen, my brother has just phoned to say he intends coming for the weekend,' Jasper said. 'Apparently, he's booked a room at a hotel nearby, but he feels it's time to think about getting back into harness and obviously wants to go over a lot of things.' He paused. 'Could you make sure that the bursar is available for a few hours tomorrow, or Sunday?' he added.

Helen smiled. 'I do hope that coming back won't be too much of a culture shock for him,' she said lightly. 'He's had quite a long time away—but we've managed, between us, haven't we?' she added.

Ria glanced at Helen, her eyes softening at the thought of the woman's life—fulfilled in one way, because she clearly looked on the school as her family, but so unfulfilled in another. Rather like her own, Ria thought, wondering for a second whether there was anyone in the whole world who could have it all. Who had a realistic hope of being settled, of finding true and lasting happiness.

The two left Jasper's room and walked swiftly down the corridor together.

Ria glanced at her watch. 'I'll have to fly—I should be in class in one minute,' she said.

'Yes, I know, it's all go in this place, isn't it?' Helen said happily. 'And now, with Carl dropping in on us unexpectedly, we'll all have to see that things are up to scratch. Jasper will be on to everyone like a ton of bricks!'

Just before midday, Carl arrived at the school and called in at Helen's office for a minute. And, when she saw him, she acknowledged a wave of surprise at his appearance. He looked different—totally different, she thought. For one thing, he seemed about ten years younger than usual, his normally close-cropped hair exchanged for a more debonair looser style around his ears, and he looked generally toned and tanned—perhaps everyone should have time off the treadmill, Helen thought. Then she suddenly realized something else— he was no longer wearing glasses, and now his deep, dark eyes were visible for all to see. She swallowed and got to her feet hurriedly.

'Carl—how lovely to see you,' she said, offering him her hand in greeting before being nearly bowled over when he caught hold of her by the shoulders and hugged her. That was the first time in fifteen years that she had been touched by her employer—in that way!

'Great to see you, too, Helen,' he said, letting her go. 'I did ring my brother earlier—is he free this morning?'

'Of course—he's waiting for you,' Helen replied.

'Well, there's no need for you to show me the way to my room,' Carl said, smiling, before departing to make his way down the corridor. After he'd gone Helen realized that she actually felt rather shattered. Something had happened to Carl Trent, she thought—he seemed to be a different man! So relaxed!

Not bothering to knock, Carl opened the headmaster's door and went inside. And Jasper sprang to his feet and came over to greet his brother, shaking his hand vigorously.

'What…where are your glasses?' he asked at once. Carl looked so unlike himself.

'Ah, well—I was persuaded by a couple of friends to have laser treatment for my short sight,' Carl said. 'Glasses do hamper things like swimming and skiing, so I woke up one morning and thought—why not?' He smiled, and for the first time in his life Jasper saw something of himself in his brother's eyes, in his expression.

'Being without them suits you,' Jasper said. He paused. 'Your holiday has done you good, Carl. You look very well. I hope you feel up to taking over again after the summer.'

''Course I do,' Carl said, 'and once you've given me all the gen, everything that's going on, what's in the pipeline, I'll be ready for anything.' He leaned back in his chair and stretched his hands above his head. 'The lovely Helen seems as usual—that woman hasn't changed a bit from the person we took on all that time ago. Still as efficient, obviously?'

'Totally,' Jasper replied at once. 'She's made it easy for me.'

For the next couple of hours the two men discussed some of the important details that needed going over, before making their way over to inspect the science block, which had been newly decorated, and to stop and have a chat now and again to one or two members of staff who happened to pass by.

Jasper suddenly looked at his watch. 'I didn't realize what the time was,' he said. 'Sorry, Carl, we've missed lunch I'm afraid.'

'Well, why don't we go to The Lamb for a bite?' Carl suggested. 'I might as well get back to the routine straight away!'

Jasper shot his brother a quick glance. To say that Carl seemed to have lightened up was an understatement.

It was almost five o'clock before they left the pub and got into Jasper's car to go back to the school, and as he drove slowly along he saw Ria just leaving the farm shop. He pulled up slowly, lowering the window.

'Want a lift, Ria?' he called, glancing at the two or three brown paper bags she was carrying.

She looked up. 'Oh—it's OK, thanks,' she said, adding, 'it'll do me good to stretch my legs and have some air.' But, just as Jasper was about to drive away again, one of the bags in her hand gave way and some fruit spilled out and fell to the ground.

He stopped at once and got out to help her pick up the plums she'd bought—one of which was obviously overripe. 'I think you'd better change your mind and hop in,' he said, glancing down at her. 'You don't want to go leaving a trail of your shopping all the way back.' He paused. 'Besides, there's someone in the car who'd like to meet you,' he said.

Obediently, Ria got into the back of the car, and Carl turned around to greet her as Jasper introduced them.

'I hear that you're helping us out at the moment,' Carl said, swallowing hard as he stared at her and, glancing across, Jasper was immediately struck by his brother's reaction. Carl was most certainly showing an interest in Ria! For a fleeting, ridiculous moment, Jasper felt a wave of resentment flow through him.

He turned to glance briefly at Ria, thinking how much better she looked now than she had that morning. A full day's teaching had obviously taken her mind off her problems…and off everything else, he thought.

As he accelerated away, he wished that Carl hadn't decided to come this weekend—there was still plenty of time to sort things out before they both reverted to their normal way of life. In Jasper's present somewhat disturbed state of mind, the last thing he felt like doing was entering into the dreary business of discussing school stuff with his brother.

Crashing in on his thoughts, Carl suddenly said, 'By the way, you may not know this, Jasper, but it's Helen's birthday on Sunday. I usually send her some flowers, but I thought she's obviously been so good during my absence it would be nice to take her out somewhere for a meal, just for a change. The chef at the hotel I'm staying at has an excellent reputation.' He paused, darting a glance back at Ria. 'Why don't we make it a foursome—it'd be more fun, wouldn't it?'

Jasper bit his lip, surprised at what Carl had just said. 'Does Helen know yet?' he asked.

'No, but I don't expect her to refuse,' Carl replied airily. He turned again to look at Ria. 'Are you free, Ria?' he asked.

Shooting a quick glance at Jasper, but unable to think quickly enough for an excuse, Ria said vaguely, 'Um… well…yes—I think so.'

'Good. Then that's settled. I'll book us in for dinner at eight.'

Presently, back in her room, Ria put her shopping away before flopping down in a chair and resting her head back. From the little she'd been told, Carl Trent did not match her preconceptions about him at all. She had expected an introverted, bookish, shy type, yet his initial handclasp had been much more intimate than she'd have expected from a complete stranger and he'd also just included her in an invitation to an extravagant meal somewhere. She closed her eyes for a second, comparing the two brothers. There was certainly a resemblance between them, but Jasper was taller, more broad-shouldered…more…seductive.

Ria's eyes flew open at that last unwelcome thought and she gritted her teeth, taking her mobile from her bag. How on earth was she going to get through the rest of her time at Highbridge Manor? she asked herself. It was all very well trying to convince Jasper that she was actually impervious to his masculine charms, but the really important thing was— could she convince herself?

She dialled Hannah's number—she needed to hear her friend's straightforward wisdom and Hannah would be home now, after being away for a week on a course.

'Hannah? Can I see you tomorrow—just for a few hours?' Ria asked eagerly.

There was barely a moment's hesitation before Hannah replied coolly, 'What's the matter, Ria?'

Ria hesitated. 'I can't discuss it over the phone,' she said.

'Then come now, tonight,' Hannah said briskly. 'I'm not doing anything tomorrow.' She recognized straight away that something was going on—recognized the telltale sound of Ria's recurring depression, the depression which was threatening to spoil her life.

'Oh, thanks, Hannah,' Ria said. She paused. 'It's just…I had dinner with my father and…and Diana…yesterday evening.' She swallowed. 'And there's so much I have to tell you,' she added softly.

CHAPTER SEVEN

AT JUST after midnight on Sunday, Jasper unbuckled his trousers and wrenched his shirt over his head before going into his bathroom to switch on the shower.

The evening had been surreal in a way, he thought, as he stared at himself in the mirror for a second—and he didn't know whether he'd enjoyed it or not.

He had to admit that the meal had been excellent, the hotel's ambience very pleasant and welcoming. But he realized how long it had been since he and Carl had spent an evening like that together—and certainly not in the company of two women. In fact, to Jasper's knowledge, Carl had never had a serious relationship...but he seemed to have learned quickly during his absence from the school environment and had been charming and attentive to Ria and Helen all evening.

Jasper paused, wiping away some condensation from the mirror with the back of his hand thoughtfully. Being away had changed his brother. There was no doubt about that and, not for the first time, Jasper felt an undeniable twinge of guilt. Long before he'd finished at university, he had boldly declared that he had no intention of committing himself to Highbridge Manor, and that, for him, the outside world was the one he intended to inhabit. Which had meant that Carl, that much older, had been obliged to fill the gap left by their father after the older man's health had started to fail. Whichever way you looked at it, Jasper thought, he'd been selfish to leave everything to Carl. He should have at least offered to shoulder some of the burden, some of the family expectations.

But, anyway, Jasper consoled himself as he stood under the shower and let the hot water run over his strong, agile body, Carl had never expected—or had never seemed to want—any other life. He had slipped into it as easily as putting on a favourite, familiar pair of shoes. And it had always worked so brilliantly. The school had continued to function as expertly as it always had. So why was he, Jasper, feeling so conscience-stricken?

Towelling himself briefly, he walked, naked, into his bedroom, knowing the answer to that last question. Because it was quite obvious just how much benefit and enjoyment Carl had derived from being away. His brother had glimpsed the apparent freedom of the outside world, during which he had obviously fully recovered from his health problems—and he'd also quickly learned how to treat women!

Helen had, naturally, been almost overwhelmed by this evening's unexpected treat—and she'd looked different, too, Jasper thought. At school, she was always groomed and well turned out, but tonight she'd chosen to wear a surprisingly low-cut floral dress and she'd left her hair loose, with a sparkly clip pinned to one side. And she'd been excited and lively.

But it was Ria who'd attracted the glances from other diners—and from Carl, who clearly found her fascinating. Jasper had spotted that all the evening. She had worn a floaty caramel-gold calf-length dress and had pinned her hair up, Grecian style. To him, she'd resembled a graceful figurine which might crumble and disappear if treated roughly. But it was her expressive hazel eyes—fringed by those long, dark lashes and always looking as if they were about to melt into tremulous tears—which drew immediate attention…igniting private sensitivities in the opposite sex and attracting them to her like moths to a light.

And it was no use denying that she had inflamed his own passionate instincts—once again—Jasper thought as he threw himself down on the bed and lay with his hands behind his head. He stared up at the ceiling. He couldn't quite believe that when they had been sitting, the four of them, in that dining room earlier, he'd actually felt jealous that he was having to share her with the others…with Carl. If it was clear that his brother had changed—fairly dramatically—it was also clear to Jasper that something had happened to *him*, too. Ever since Ria had appeared on the scene, he didn't feel like the same person who had managed to step so skilfully into Carl's shoes. And, despite all his determination and reservations about the female sex, he knew beyond doubt that he needed a woman—a woman of his own. But how could he have fallen for it again, after everything that had happened? And with a member of his staff! He knew he was on a roller coaster this time but he'd sort it, one way or the other, until he'd convinced himself that he could let her go in a few weeks' time and never see her or think of her again.

He got off the bed and padded over to pour himself a whisky. That last thought was an impossibility, he thought, because Ria fell into a very select category.

Unforgettable.

But, since there were less than six weeks to go before the end of the school year, before she set off into the unknown on her travels, he had better keep his mind firmly on his job— the end of which was fast approaching. He had never become interested emotionally in any other member of his staff before—either here or at his factory—had never had his feelings stirred before. Not like this.

He swallowed the whisky in one gulp. It was time for some clear thinking.

On Monday morning, Carl called back to the school to say goodbye before leaving to return to the house in the Lake District he'd been sharing with friends for the last few weeks.

'I shan't be back until the final Awards ceremonies—when you shut up shop,' he said cheerily to Jasper. 'Meanwhile, keep up the good work!'

As he drove out of sight, Jasper admitted to a feeling of relief that his brother had gone. During their long discussions over the weekend, there had been moments when he'd felt surprisingly edgy during Carl's visit—their lifelong competitiveness seeming to re-emerge. But Carl had been very understanding about the debacle over Ria's predecessor.

'Oh, that could have happened to me,' he'd said. 'It's not always easy to see the wood for the trees during the interviewing process—but you did exactly the right thing in dispensing with the woman's services. And, anyway, if you hadn't had to sack her, you'd never have come across Ria, would you? Think what we'd have missed!' He'd paused. 'Can't you persuade her to stay on next year, Jaz? When she was talking about her plans to travel I didn't think she sounded all that enthusiastic. She'd be a terrific asset on the permanent staff, wouldn't she? Use all your masculine powers of seduction to get her to agree—you know you can do it—and you'd be doing me a favour because I liked her. A lot.'

On the following Friday afternoon, after finishing the last lesson of the day, Ria left the classroom and made her way up the stairs to her flat, humming a little tune to herself.

She'd felt so much happier this week—about everything, she thought. Spending those few hours last weekend with Hannah, being allowed to spill out all her feelings and taking on board all her friend's comments and common sense had done her the world of good. It was Hannah, after all, who knew all the details of Ria's background, and Hannah was the only one who she would ever tell about what had happened the other night after she'd got back from seeing her father and Diana. And Hannah hadn't teased her when Ria had described the way Jasper Trent had kissed her so fully—so completely—and so unexpectedly out of character. She had merely raised her eyebrows thoughtfully and opened another bottle of wine.

Today, Ria had initiated her poetry ideas with the fourteen-year-olds—and they'd seemed interested and enthusiastic. There had only been time towards the end of the lesson to have a brief discussion about what they'd cover, but Ria had been gratified to learn that several boys were able to quote lines from well-known sonnets and poems, apparently familiar with the most popular ones—many of which were her own favourites. This realization had given her a real buzz—so it wasn't all maths and sport and IT, after all, she thought happily. And she was surprised that a few of the more mature pupils—already more men than boys—seemed particularly eager to devote a whole lesson to poetry. She might have expected them to yawn widely at the very idea. But chatting about her favourite subject had been a lovely way to end a busy week, Ria thought, as she unlocked her door. It had been like a tonic.

Presently, after she'd showered and changed into her hipster jeans and a fresh top, Ria decided to have a picnic in the little wood that lay beyond the cricket green. It was a blissfully warm evening and she decided she would take one or two of her poetry books and start planning next week's exercise.

Going over to the window, she saw troops of boys making their way off the premises towards the coaches which would be waiting at the entrance of the school to take them to Salisbury for an outing to the theatre. She smiled as she saw the last of them disappear from sight. It was going to be very quiet here this evening! With a little stab of surprise, she realized just how quickly she had melded into the fabric of this place, how much she had been made to feel necessary and indispensable. And wanted.

Turning away, she shook her head briefly. She was going to miss all this, the children, the atmosphere. She was going to miss being part of this family.

On the top of the fridge, she spotted one or two bags which certainly hadn't been purchased by her and, opening them, she saw two soft bread rolls, two delicious slices of gammon ham and a little carton of dressed salad, plus two still-warm custard Danish pastries. Claudia had been her fairy godmother once again, Ria thought gratefully. They had only had the opportunity for a few fleeting chats during the time Ria had been at the school, but the housekeeper seemed to know exactly what—and how much—Ria liked to eat without being asked or expected to provide any of it for her. It was as if she had taken Ria under her wing and when she left the school, she thought as she packed her picnic into a plastic box, she'd buy Claudia a really special thank you present.

Ria filled her small Thermos flask with coffee, then tucked everything into her rucksack—not forgetting to include her notebook and pen. She was feeling so upbeat this evening, she might even write some more lines of her own later, she thought.

She paused, staring into space for a moment. She realized that she had barely seen Jasper at all since Sunday's outing to the hotel. And during the whole of that evening he had treated her no differently than he'd treated Helen—he'd been courteous and attentive, but no more than that. And not once had they exchanged anything that could be described as an intimate glance, or gesture, that might remind them of their passionate encounter the other night. It was as if it had never happened. And, anyway, he'd explained the reason for it clearly enough. He'd felt sorry for her, that was all. Ria shrugged. It was obvious that he had completely forgotten all about it—to him, it was probably par for the course and not worth a second thought.

She took a long, deep breath. It was true that concentrating on her teaching had helped her get through the last few days, had allowed her to function normally. But if she thought that she would ever, *ever* forget the magical moment when Jasper had held her so intimately, she was kidding herself.

It took only seven or eight minutes to reach the copse and, looking around her, Ria noticed the remains of a sawn-off tree trunk. Great! That would be useful to rest her pad on. She plonked herself down by the side, where the ground was mossy and not at all damp, and the evening sunlight shafting through the bushes bathed everything in a mellow light. If you weren't inspired to compose here, Ria thought, you couldn't compose anywhere.

Leaning back on her elbows, she lifted her head upwards and closed her eyes for a few seconds, suddenly feeling drowsy. There had been no free time out of lessons today and she was tired—but she never minded this sort of fulfilled tiredness. It was a pleasant feeling. A contented feeling.

'Do you mind if I join you?'

Jasper's voice catapulted Ria from her reverie. In that short time, she had actually dozed off and, opening her eyes quickly, she looked up to see his tall frame almost cutting out the light. He was wearing jeans and a polo shirt, and he stood with his hands in his pockets, scrutinizing her calmly.

'I've just been inspecting the cricket green for tomorrow,' he said briefly. 'I saw you walking over here.'

He sat down alongside her and glanced across. 'It's much too fine an evening to stay inside—and I'm very glad I decided not to go on the theatre trip tonight,' he said.

Ria sat up properly. 'I was in two minds whether to take the opportunity,' she said, 'but I thought I'd use the time doing some work, instead.'

'Very noble.' He smiled.

'Oh, I'm not being noble,' Ria answered at once. 'The work I'm talking about is all pleasure.' She patted the bag containing her books. 'It's all about the poetry session I intend doing with Class Four and I thought a couple of hours, with no chance of any interruption, might be useful.' Then, realizing what she'd just said, she put her hand to her mouth apologetically. 'Sorry—I meant from the children…'

He grinned across at her. 'I promise to be extremely quiet,' he said.

How very informally polite they were being, Ria thought, now that they were alone together for the first time since he'd apologized for kissing her. There was nothing in his expression to suggest that it had crossed his mind since—and how was *she* managing to appear so casual…so completely normal? She'd even stopped herself from blushing, which must be a first.

To cover her silent confusion, she said, 'I've brought a picnic. Dear Claudia must have known exactly what I would like.' She paused, the mood she was in giving her courage. 'Would you like to share it?' she asked. 'There's plenty.'

'I was actually going to go to The Lamb for dinner later,'

he said, 'and, anyway, it's not fair to keep eating your stuff.' But he knew he would be accepting her offer. And, anyway, treating her as he would any other member of staff was the sensible way to go—keep things ordinary, uncomplicated. He would never give her cause again to think that she was someone special…

'It's perfectly fair to share,' Ria contradicted lightly, opening her rucksack and taking out the picnic. 'It's funny,' she said, as she set the food on to a large piece of kitchen roll on her lap, 'I didn't mean to pack everything Claudia left for me because there's far too much of it.' She glanced up at him briefly. 'I must have known that someone might turn up.'

He didn't reply to that, and presently they munched away at the ham rolls, into which Ria had added some of the salad, lifting it carefully in place with the little plastic spoon provided.

Presently, she said, 'I'm afraid the coffee I've brought isn't the kind you like—it's got milk and sugar.'

He shook his head. 'No, I'm fine thanks, Ria—you carry on. And you can eat both the pastries. Sweet things aren't my particular taste.'

He'd finished his roll in a couple of moments and sat with his legs stretched out, watching her covertly as she nibbled at the cake and sipped her coffee. She was enchanting, he decided. She had cast a spell over him which he knew was going to be hard to shake off. He cleared his throat.

'Tell me about the poetry,' he said, not being able to think of anything else to say. 'What have you got in mind?'

'Well, for a start, I've asked the boys to bring along one of their own favourites—and I was surprised how knowledge-able some of them were,' she said. 'I've told them it can be anything—Shakespeare, or the War Poets, or Nonsense Rhymes—anything that triggers their interest and imagi-nation. And they will be expected to read out whatever they bring along, so that we can all enjoy it.'

Ria put the picnic things away and sat hugging her knees. 'And if there's time before the end of term, we'll see if any of them can compose something of their own. Just four lines or so, in the style they prefer—nothing too onerous.'

She smiled up at him, her eyes bright, and he smiled back at her slowly. Carl was right, he thought. She would be an undoubted asset to the school if she stayed on.

'I hope you're not expecting anything from me,' he said. 'Poetry has never been my thing, I'm afraid, but I can quite understand how it entrances and intrigues the more aesthetic amongst us.' He paused. 'I'd like to know what your own favourites are, Ria,' he said, and she responded at once.

'Oh, I've masses of favourites!' she said. 'Rupert Brooke, of course…and Wordsworth and Christina Rossetti—' She paused. 'But it's Elizabeth Barrett Browning who has a special place in my long, long list…'

'And I expect you know many of them by heart?' Jasper ventured.

'Well, I have spent a lot of my life reading them, again and again,' Ria said.

There was silence for a moment, then Jasper said, 'Read me your all-time favourite, Ria—read it aloud. Let's see if I can enjoy it, too.' At least talking about school was keeping things on a level footing, he thought.

Ria caught her breath and looked away for a second. 'Oh, I don't want to bore you,' she said, hoping he'd forget it. But he didn't.

'Please,' he said. 'I would really like to hear you read aloud.'

Well, after going on about it like she had, she could hardly refuse him, Ria thought. And, anyway, why not? She would enjoy reciting those words again—for about the millionth time in her life.

Suddenly, all her shyness evaporated and in a low but steady voice she began…

"'How do I love thee? Let me count the ways. I love thee to the depth and breadth and height My soul can reach, when feeling out of sight…'"

Ria's gentle tones caressed the words as she continued on to the end…

"'I love thee freely, as men strive for Right; I love thee purely, as they turn from Praise. I love thee with the passion put to use In my old griefs, and with my childhood's faith…'"

Here, Ria's voice broke slightly as she struggled to contain her emotions…

"'I love thee with a love I seemed to lose With my lost saints, I love thee with the breath, Smiles, tears of all my life! and, if God choose, I shall but love thee better after death.'"

Ria's voice trailed off as she came to the closing words, and for a few moments neither of them spoke.

It was abundantly clear to Jasper that this particular poem held special resonance for Ria and, studying her face, which was pale and expressionless with no hint of tears in her eyes, made him want to take her in his arms, enfold her to him and kiss her moist lips deeply. He sighed inwardly. Her own sensitivities were infectious, and the way she had spoken those lines had touched him in a surprising way.

He was the first to speak and, when he did, his voice was gruff. 'You almost carried me away there, Ria,' he murmured. 'I have a very distant memory of that poem myself, but it never impressed me as you managed to do just then.'

She turned slowly to look at him, and he knew that for those few moments Ria had been in another world.

They sat there for another half an hour or so, talking about general things, but Ria's mood had changed significantly—and Jasper felt that somehow that was his fault. He shouldn't have asked her to recite that poem. He had intruded into her secret life, and he had no right to do it. He made a sudden decision.

'Look, I know I've ruined all your plans to be by yourself and do some work tonight, Ria,' he said, 'but I need a drink, and you're coming with me.' He stood up and pulled her to her feet, and for a second their bodies moulded together as she looked up at him. And his masculine warmth seemed to wash over her like a comforting, reassuring tide.

'All right,' she said, as if she had no choice in the matter. 'Anyway, the sun's gone down and I was beginning to get cold. And I don't feel like doing any more work now, in any case.'

He grinned down at her as she stooped to gather her things together, and as she straightened up he put a hand on her waist to steady her on the uneven ground.

'We won't go to The Lamb,' he said briefly. 'It'll be too crowded on a Friday night. I know somewhere else which will be quieter.'

CHAPTER EIGHT

SITTING on a rather ancient wicker chair by the window, Ria watched as Jasper stood over at the bar giving their order for dinner. She felt so relieved that their relationship had returned to where it had been before, with neither of them apparently giving their emotional 'blip' another thought. They seemed happy and comfortable with each other, she thought, with no bothersome undercurrents.

The Three Horseshoes was a surprisingly old-fashioned pub, with no smart fittings and furnishings, and no music or fruit machines. With its oak settles and one or two wooden pews obviously rescued from a derelict church, it felt in a sort of time-warp. But, despite this—or because of it—there were enough customers to give the place the air of a comfortable, well-liked venue. And Ria instinctively knew that it would be Jasper's kind of place, that he would enjoy coming here. It was a no-nonsense, no-frills enterprise, but he'd assured her that the food—and the beer—were wonderful.

Having already eaten her ham roll and one of the pastries, Ria wasn't hungry so she'd asked for a small portion of king prawns and salad—but it was obvious that Jasper would need something more substantial.

Presently, he brought over their drinks and sat down opposite her.

'One of the reasons I like coming here from time to time,' he said casually, 'is because no one from school ever does—well, not to my knowledge.' He lifted his pint of beer to his lips and drank freely, and Ria looked away for a second, feeling awkward at what he'd just said. Maybe he didn't want the two of them to be seen together, off duty. She could well imagine that what Jasper Trent did in his own time, and away from school, he liked to keep private. To avoid unnecessary gossip.

Raising her eyes as she sipped at her glass of dry white wine, Ria found him gazing at her with such an odd expression on his face that she was forced to look away quickly.

'Carl was very interested in what I'll be doing in a few months' time,' she said lightly, 'and he's given me his mobile number so that I can contact him if I need any advice, or if I have any queries.' She paused. 'He seems to have done a lot of travelling himself while he's been away.'

Jasper felt a moment of irritation at her words. Carl had learned something about opportunism, he thought. His brother knew only too well that if Ria needed any advice she need look no further than Jasper himself, who'd travelled widely, both in business and for pleasure. Moving his glass out of the way, he leaned forward for a moment, his elbows on the table.

'Don't bother to ask Carl about your plans,' he said bluntly. 'I can give you the gen about most of the civilized world.' He paused. 'Are you…are you still going ahead with your travelling?' he asked casually. 'You haven't changed your mind? Reconsidered?'

'Why do you ask that?'

'Oh, it's just that you've fitted in so brilliantly at Highbridge Manor, I thought you may like to give yourself more time to think things over…perhaps postpone the idea, anyway,' he said.

Ria felt a small thrill of pleasure at what he'd just said. It was always good to be appreciated…and especially by someone like Jasper Trent.

She had leaned forward, too, now, and their faces were so close she could feel his breath, just faintly, on her cheek. She was never likely to meet another man like him if she lived to be a hundred. He was so handsome, she thought helplessly, to a point that could barely be described, and although she was trying desperately hard to stop her imagination, her thoughts, from running away with her, to be alone with him like this filled her with an air of such breathless intensity she felt slightly faint. *Why* had their paths crossed? she asked herself again. She didn't *want* to feel this way about a man—any man—ever again. She had set her heart on other things. But being forced into such close proximity with this perfect example of British masculinity was making things unutterably difficult for her. And the painful truth was that she knew how much she envied the woman in his life, who was obviously important to him, special to him. Life was so cruel. *She* could never be special—although all her emotions were tricking her into thinking otherwise.

She picked up her glass again, knowing that her hand was trembling, and knowing that he saw it.

'I have no intention of changing my plans—at the moment,' she said guardedly. 'But it's very gratifying that you should want me to stay on next year, Jasper.'

He raised one eyebrow. 'It was Carl's idea,' he said flatly. 'And of course it won't matter to me because I'll be well out of here, in any case.'

Ria came back down to earth with a bump. What on earth had made her think that he cared that much about her? She had set her foot on a path familiar to many vulnerable women, she thought grimly—getting the wrong end of the stick.

Hoping for the impossible. His remarks had been all about the practicalities of running the school, and nothing at all to do with personal wishes or preferences…or feelings.

Just then the waiter arrived with their meal and, although the large prawns and the garlic dip looked very appealing, Ria knew that she had suddenly lost what little appetite she had. And, glancing up as Jasper slid his knife into the succulent rare steak he'd ordered, Ria knew that she had to face one unpalatable fact. She had actually fallen in love again. It was no use denying it, and the thought made her feel empty, worried—and angry. All her plans to travel had nothing at all to do with an unusual spirit of adventure on her part…of going away. It was everything to do with *running* away—running away from her old life and its unsolvable problems. But what had made her think that it would work? That it would solve anything? Never mind travelling from Tanzania to Timbuktu, her short journey from London to Hampshire had demonstrated an awkward point—that she might try escaping from love and all its hurts but it would catch her up every time. It would find her, wherever she happened to be.

'Oh, by the way,' she said, picking up one of the prawns by her finger and thumb and dipping it into the garlic sauce, 'I made a point of talking to Josh about the tennis question—and he was *so* relieved. So grateful.' She smiled. 'It was sweet, really. I felt as if I'd given him an extra-special present of some sort.'

Jasper cut into his steak again and glanced up at her.

'Well, you did, didn't you,' he said. 'You took his problem on board, took it seriously and did something about it.' He paused for a second. 'Poor little devil. He's not used to being given such consideration—and you made him feel as if he mattered.'

Ria looked across at Jasper steadily, wondering whether he'd be prepared to tell her about Josh's background. She decided to take the risk of a rebuttal.

'What's going on in his life?' she asked. 'Why was he sent away from home at such an awkward time of the year?'

Jasper hesitated for only a second before replying. Unless it was essential, he never discussed his pupils' personal situations with the staff. Tell one person, and you've told ten, he always maintained, and privacy should be respected. It was exactly the view he took with his staff at the factory.

But it was different with Ria Davidson. He knew, without it being specifically proved, that she could be trusted implicitly, in any matter, to be discreet. And somehow he felt that she deserved to be told about Josh.

Ria listened in growing dismay. 'Oh, poor Josh,' she said quietly. 'Now I know why he likes to stay on after class and talk—he's such a sensitive little thing. And he seems to hang on to my every word,' she added.

Jasper nodded. 'Yes, and your attitude towards him is part of what I'm talking about,' he said. 'You're happy to give him some of your time, and that helps his self-belief—which is in short supply.'

Jasper put down his knife and fork and picked up his glass. 'One thing I've learned in the last year is how hard it is for some children. I mean, surely, if you decide to have kids they should become your personal responsibility from the word go, and they should always hold prime position in your life afterwards, shouldn't they? Children don't ask to be born, and their happiness should come first, be above anything else. Self-serving, selfish parents are the pits in my book.' Jasper's mouth twisted angrily. 'Some people appear to be quite happy giving life to a child—as long as it doesn't affect their own lives afterwards. That's when far too many seem to lose interest.'

Ria picked up her own glass and looked away for a second. Jasper's words had sent a cold shiver down her spine... How would *she* rate, in his opinion? Not that the question would ever be answered, because he was never going to know what had happened in her own past. That was her secret, and one which would always bore a painful hole in her conscience, however hard Hannah tried to persuade her to stop torturing herself.

There was silence for a few moments after that, then Jasper looked across at her.

'You obviously weren't as hungry as I was,' he said, glancing down at his empty plate. 'But, of course, I declined that very attractive pastry, didn't I.'

Ria smiled quickly. 'The prawns were great, Jasper,' she said, 'but I couldn't manage any more.'

He studied her thoughtfully for a few seconds. She had that lost expression in her eyes again—that expression that always got to him. He made a sudden decision, and cleared his throat.

'You may not realize it, but next weekend is our version of half-term,' he said briefly. 'It amounts to Friday and Monday tacked onto either side.' He paused. 'If you're not otherwise engaged, why don't you come to Somerset with me? I like to have people around sometimes, and I've got into the habit of inviting friends and colleagues to the cottage for a break now and again.'

Ria was almost bowled over by the unexpectedness of the suggestion, and she swallowed. 'What…what happens to the pupils?'

'Oh, they always stay put. Do whatever they like—but no work, unless they insist on it, which I don't think any of them ever have. All sorts of activities are arranged for them by an agency we've used for years. Only the sports staff stay on to help supervise, and of course the domiciliary staff are always on hand. It's been a tradition at the school for a long time, and the kids look forward to it.' Jasper drained his glass and sat back. 'There are sports activities, there are some films on offer, and there's always a barbecue and a disco, so no one gets bored or feels at a loose end.'

'Do none of the boys go home?' Ria asked.

'We don't encourage it because there's not really time, and it would be too disruptive,' Jasper said. 'And no one seems to want to, anyway,' he added. 'They don't want to miss out on anything. But it always seems to give the boys a real restoration break, and then we all sail on, refreshed, to the end of term.'

He finished his beer. 'So—would you like to come?' he asked bluntly.

Ria waited a long moment. She didn't know whether this was a good idea or not—the issue of his partner at home still hadn't been cleared up.

'Well—wouldn't I be rather in the way?' she asked.

He frowned. 'Why should you be? I've also invited a couple of my employees along as well, and I wouldn't have suggested you coming if I thought you'd be in the way.' He shrugged. 'I just thought that a complete change of scene… change of air…might do you good. It always does *me* good,' he added, 'but it's entirely up to you.'

Anxious not to appear ungracious, Ria smiled quickly. She suddenly remembered that Hannah wouldn't be at home because she was going to visit her parents up north—so Ria would be alone for the four-day break. Anyway, she admitted to being very curious to see Jasper's no doubt amazingly fantastic cottage in the country, and to meet the woman in his life.

'I'd…I'd love to come,' she said. 'Thanks. Thanks very much.'

'Good,' he said. 'We'll leave as soon as we can after classes finish on Thursday evening.'

Presently, they drove back to Highbridge Manor, Jasper deliberately not hurrying because he didn't want the evening to end. But he did wonder, briefly, whether he'd done the right thing in inviting her to the cottage. It had been a spontaneous suggestion on his part, made without thinking. And was it for her benefit, as he'd said, or for his own? And he knew the answer to that. Then he shrugged inwardly. Where the female sex was concerned, he had developed a very satisfactory suit of armour which he would permit to be dented only up to a point—the point at which he could turn back and switch off again. Well, that was what all men did, didn't they?

As they parted company for the night, Jasper said, 'By the way, in case I forget to mention it again, pack a swimsuit next weekend. Debra will have made sure that the water in the pool is just the right temperature, whatever the weather.'

CHAPTER NINE

BY THE time they were ready to leave on Thursday evening, it was past seven o'clock, and Jasper turned to glance at Ria as she fastened her seat belt.

'I'd hoped to get away before this,' he remarked casually, 'but there are always important details to be sorted at the last minute.' He didn't bother to add that he'd deliberately waited until Helen was safely off the premises first... Idle suppositions did no one any good—well, did *him* no good.

As if her mind was on the same track, Ria said, 'Helen told me that her mother has been much better these last couple of weeks, so she is actually going away for a couple of days' break, too, with some friends. They've booked a log cabin in one of the Forestry Commission holiday places in Wales.'

Jasper raised his eyes briefly. 'That's a first,' he said casually. 'Well, I hope they have a good time. Helen is a hard worker and a terrific asset to Highbridge Manor. She deserves some time to herself.'

Ria waited a moment. 'I didn't tell her where I was going,' she said, looking out of the passenger window. She paused. 'I thought...I thought it would be better not to.'

'OK, fine,' he said. Tact was a great asset, and Ria seemed to have plenty of that, he thought. And, anyway, he'd known that she'd keep quiet about it. Far safer, for both of them.

It was nine-thirty by the time they reached the small hamlet a few miles outside Bath where Jasper's cottage was situated, and Ria's heart rate had increased considerably at the thought of meeting his woman friend. She'd already formed a picture in her mind of Debra—who would be tall, raven-haired and wearing immaculate make-up, she thought. Also supremely assured and sophisticated. Everything that *she* wasn't.

'Debra's going to fix supper—she knew we'd be late,' Jasper remarked casually, 'so at least we won't be eating at a pub tonight.'

Almost at once after he'd said that, he indicated left and began driving slowly along a short grassy track, at the end of which was a single building, standing entirely alone. There were no other dwellings in sight.

'Well, here we are.' Jasper brought the car to a standstill. 'This is where I recharge my batteries.'

Ria drew in her breath in silent admiration as she took in the sight. Lavender Cottage was a sturdy building, its stone-tiled roof and chimney pots indicating its ancient provenance. The heavy blue-painted front door had a single brass knocker and the three windows above it, and the two either side of it, were latticed. The lawns flanking the short drive were well kept, the borders filled with shrubs and old-fashioned plants. To Ria, the cottage seemed as if it had been dropped there from another century.

'What a beautiful place, Jasper,' she said simply. 'No wonder you like escaping here.'

He got out of the car and came around to open her door, grinning down at her as she stepped out. 'I have to admit that you are seeing it at a wonderful time of year,' he said. 'Surrounded by these hills, it can look pretty bleak in winter. But it never feels bleak to me.'

The front door led straight into an elegant lounge, which was bathed in a mellow light from several lighted table lamps, and Jasper went forward to open another door which would lead to the rest of the house.

'I don't think Debra is in,' he said, 'or the door would have been open. Never mind—she won't be long.'

They went together across the narrow hallway, coming at once to another room, beyond which was a conservatory—and Ria found it hard not to gasp out loud. It was huge by any standards, its double doors open wide to reveal a spectacular garden patio leading to a kidney-shaped swimming pool. And the whole scene was gently illuminated by discreet lighting, causing shifting shadows to catch the eye.

Ria just stood for a moment, not wanting to say too much— or too little. Of course, she'd known that Jasper Trent must be fabulously wealthy, and she shouldn't really have been surprised at his country property. But the sight of all the expensive furnishings, the décor, the opulence, was almost overwhelming. She sighed inwardly, confessing that she would love to live here. It was everything anyone could wish for.

'I'll just fetch our stuff from the car,' Jasper said. 'Sit down—have a look around—make yourself at home, Ria. Shan't be a minute.'

As she wandered outside, the balmy early June air—still comfortably warm, even this late—wafted the scent of roses towards Ria, filling her nostrils with their perfume, and after a moment she sat down on one of the chairs by the pool, wishing that she could hold the moment for ever. It was bliss, she thought, and one of those experiences when she wished that time would stand still and that the clock would stop.

Suddenly, a voice behind her said, 'Hello, there,' and, getting up quickly, Ria found herself face to face with a short,

fairly rounded woman with grey hair framing a pleasant uncomplicated face. 'I'm Debra—and of course you're Ria.'
She smiled. 'Jasper told me to make myself known to you—
he's just had a phone call from the office, apparently, so he'll
be a few minutes, I expect.'

Ria smiled back, trying not to show her surprise. Well, it
was more than surprise—it was astonishment. She'd been at
it again, she thought, forming mental pictures that turned out
to be totally inaccurate. But she admitted to a feeling of
immense relief that she'd been wrong!

'This is such a lovely place, isn't it,' she said. 'It must be
wonderful to live here.'

Debra nodded, folding her arms, obviously quite ready for
a chat. 'Yes, but it wasn't always like this, you know.
Jasper's been responsible for transforming it from the rather
down-at-heel place it was when he bought it. When he
arrived, we all wondered what he was going to do with the
place—and what *he* was going to be like—but we needn't
have worried. He's a marvellous neighbour—everyone took
to him straight away.' She smiled. 'Country folk can be
rather insular at times—not always welcoming strangers.
And when he said he was looking for someone to mind the
place, to be on hand when he wasn't here—well, I offered
my services and I've been glad of it because my husband had
to take early retirement a few years ago—bad heart, I'm
afraid. We only live a few minutes' walk away, so it's no
problem.' She paused. 'Of course, Jasper hasn't been around
so much this year, because of the school. You work there,
too, don't you, but he'll be back more or less permanently
in August, I believe.'

'I didn't think he had any neighbours,' Ria said. 'It looks
very isolated to me.'

'Oh, there are seven or eight cottages, a few council

houses—and a farm—none of which you can see from here,'
Debra said. 'But we do have a small pub—and that's where
Jasper gets to keep up with everyone when he can.'

After a few moments Jasper returned, snapping his mobile
phone shut. 'Sorry about the delay,' he said. 'That was the
office. There's apparently a minor problem which needs my
attention, so I'll have to go over there tomorrow morning.' He
made a face. 'Why did I think I was going to have a few days'
peace to chill out?'

Debra looked from one to the other shrewdly, her head on
one side. Jasper had merely told her that he was bringing a
member of staff with him, someone who needed a break, and
for some reason she'd thought it would be a man—not this
beautiful young woman. Debra tried not to purse her lips. He
certainly knew how to pick them—as far as looks went, she
thought. But looks weren't everything and she hoped he'd be
more careful this time. Still, it would do him good to relax
here with someone he obviously liked, and there was no doubt
that he did like her. Debra knew all the signs. She wasn't born
yesterday.

'I've made up the beds in the room at the front, like you
asked me to, Jasper,' Debra said, and he frowned briefly.

'Great. Thanks, Debra, but we're only going to need one
room now—for Ria. That was another reason for the phone
call. Martin and Heather won't be here for the weekend, after
all. They both think they've got flu coming on.' He paused.
'How's Dave, by the way?' he added.

'Oh, ticking along, thanks. He's OK as long as he takes it
easy.' Debra turned to go. 'Supper's laid up in the kitchen,'
she said, 'and there's everything you'll need for your breakfast in the fridge.'

After she'd gone, Jasper looked down at Ria. 'Come on,'
he said. 'Let me show you where you'll be sleeping.'

* * *

Much later, after they'd eaten the thick, moist slices of baked ham and finished the perfectly cooked vegetables freshly dug from Dave's garden, Jasper and Ria sat in the conservatory, still with the doors wide open.

For the first time since she'd finished with Seth, Ria realized that she felt totally at ease with a member of the opposite sex—even if he was her employer. In fact, it was much more than that, she told herself truthfully. She felt *lucky* to be with someone like Jasper Trent—well, wouldn't any woman? He was being attentive without being smarmy, apparently appreciating her opinion on every subject which they touched on, and treating her with total respect which, under the particular circumstances, she was very thankful for. But then, she thought, trying to stop herself from feeling too complacent, something told her that he was like this with everyone—anyone he might invite to his sumptuous home. He would quite naturally be the perfect host.

They were sitting opposite each other in two deep armchairs finishing their coffee and after a moment Jasper leaned forward to pour some more wine into Ria's glass. But she put up her hand quickly.

'No more for me, thanks, Jasper,' she said. 'I've already exceeded my normal limit.' She smiled apologetically. 'I don't want to wake up with a thick head in the morning.'

He put the bottle down again. 'No, and I won't have any more, either,' he said. 'Because I intend having a midnight swim later.'

He lounged back, studying Ria, who had closed her eyes briefly. She was still dressed in the jeans and loose green kaftan top she'd travelled in, and she'd kicked off her strappy sandals and was wiggling her toes contentedly. To him, she looked fabulous and utterly appealing. How colourless life would be without women, he thought—especially beautiful women.

Funny thing, he mused—he'd always thought that Carl

was impervious to the charms of the female sex but, after seeing how lively he'd been the other night at the hotel, Jasper wasn't so sure. Maybe he and his brother weren't so different, after all. He frowned slightly as he remembered how Carl had been so obviously enchanted by Ria—and the fact that he had given her his phone number was significant. Most un-Carl-like. Leaning forward, he put his glass down on the table by his side, and Ria roused herself quickly.

'Oh, sorry…I nearly fell asleep then! How very rude of me,' she said, sitting up properly.

He raised one eyebrow. 'The reason I brought you here was so that you could wind down and really relax, even if it is for only a short time,' he said casually. 'I'm delighted that you've started to do that right away.'

She took a long, deep breath. 'I've been thinking…I've never lived anywhere that I could call home—not really. The place in London can only be described as the family bolthole. I hardly ever visit, and no one seems to sleep there for more than a few nights at a time. Apart from that, I've shared rented flats with friends.' She made a face. 'I can't imagine what it would be like to actually own somewhere, to come in and close my very own front door, knowing that it belongs to me.' She smiled briefly. 'But maybe, in a year or so, after my travelling is done and I return to my native soil, I will start looking around for somewhere…though it won't be anything like this,' she added.

Neither spoke for a few moments, then Jasper said offhandedly, 'Have you heard from your family lately?'

Ria's expression changed at once. 'I had a text from Dad—in answer to one from me,' she said briefly. 'They appear to be…very well. Very happy. Which is nice for them,' she added.

Jasper stared straight ahead of him for a moment or two. Ria's last remark had a poignant edge to it, he thought, remembering again how upset she'd been the other night. He had always known that Ria Davidson was an emotionally lonely woman—a woman who had never experienced close family ties. But she was a fully grown adult, he thought, and everyone must move on, whatever their personal problems, their personal hang-ups.

By now it was well past midnight and Jasper sat forward. 'I'm going to have a swim,' he said. 'The temperature in the pool is perfect, and letting the water take the weight from our bodies for half an hour will be wonderful.' He stood up and held out his hand. 'Come on, Ria. This is all part of the therapy.'

Ria took his hand—somewhat reluctantly at first—until she felt his fingers close firmly onto hers, sending her nerves all over the place. She had certainly not intended to swim tonight but, for some reason, the thought suddenly excited her. Swimming was a known pick-me-up. She smiled up at him quickly as she got to her feet.

'I'll get my swimsuit,' she said.

By the time Ria returned to the swimming pool, Jasper was already in the water, totally submerged and streaking up and down the length of it as if he was practising for the Olympics. She stood for a moment, watching the effortless way he moved. Suddenly he lifted his head clear of the water, shaking the hair from his eyes vigorously in order to clear his sight. Slowing down, he came over to the side where she was standing and trod water for a moment as he gazed up at her.

He had always suspected that beneath her clothes there was a perfect figure—and he was right. Ria's black bikini exquisitely sculpted her feminine curves, exhibiting an hourglass figure which most women would die for, he thought. She had partly protected her hair with a wide black band, which had the effect of outlining the perfect bone-structure of her face, the delicacy of her skin. Jasper gritted his teeth for a second. This woman had *definitely* been put on this earth to tempt him, to drive him mad, he thought. And he'd told himself—so many times—that he was beyond that. Beyond temptation. Well, he was wrong, he decided.

'Come on in,' he invited. 'You won't regret it.'

Oh, but she was regretting it already! To be here, just the two of them, on this rather magical night, and semi-clothed, was asking for trouble! But she couldn't change her mind now—and for once she couldn't have cared less. And the water did look enticing.

Sitting down carefully on the side of the pool, she dipped her toes into the water and flexed them for a moment, before sliding gracefully in and striking out. Jasper was right. It was heavenly…tepid, soothing…and totally forgiving. Yes, that was the word, she thought, as she measured her strokes rhythmically, keeping pace with Jasper, who had now come up alongside her. Warm, deep water was forgiving, understanding, buoying her up so that she felt as if she was drifting along, weightless, on an unseen cloud.

They were close together now and he turned on his side to look at her, his white teeth glistening in the semi-darkness as he smiled across.

'Well, what do you think? Is this good?' he murmured.

'Very good.' Ria smiled back. 'I think I would like to stay here for ever and I shall be tendering my resignation as soon as we go back to school.'

'Well, there's no chance that it will be accepted,' he said darkly. 'You're there until I say you can leave. You signed the contract, remember.'

They had reached the far end of the pool, and together they turned and started to swim back again, and suddenly Jasper could stand it no longer. With one strong arm, and throwing discretion and all his common sense to the wind, he pulled her towards him, and she was powerless to stop him—even if she wanted to. And Ria didn't want to… She wanted to feel his body close in on hers, wanted to feel his masculinity wrap itself around her again in that breathtakingly memorable way.

Now, as he held her against him protectively and with her hands clasped around his neck, they were twisting, swirling gently as they trod water together and, as Jasper's mouth locked on to her parted lips, his tongue searching for hers, Ria felt as if she was actually melting away, that she was going to expire until there was nothing left of her at all.

Neither of them said a word for several minutes of what was an intensely erotic experience for both of them as he released her for a second before reclaiming her lips, again and again. Ria had certainly never been in this sort of situation before, in this act of gentle lovemaking, but undoubtedly it was the sort of thing Jasper was well practised at. How many times before had he engaged in this kind of activity with other women he'd invited here? But she wasn't going to think of that. She wasn't going to spoil these intoxicating few moments… She was going to enjoy the here and now. Enjoy being desired by this alpha male whose whole persona spelt tantalizing danger.

How long they remained like that—immersed not only in the water but in each other—Ria would never know. She only thought that, as a baby in the womb, she must have felt just like that—protected in warm water, held tightly and nurtured by someone who cared only about her.

Presently, without uttering a word, they reluctantly disentangled themselves and swam to the side of the pool. Jasper heaved himself up, then held out his arms to pull Ria up alongside him, hugging her to him for the briefest of seconds before standing up and going over to collect the huge beach towels he had brought from the house. He shook one out and wrapped it around Ria's shoulders.

'There,' he said gently. 'You'll sleep like a baby tonight, Ria. I guarantee it.'

He tied his own towel around his waist, and together they went back into the house.

He glanced down at her briefly. She had pulled the band from her hair, which was now hanging down around her shoulders in tight wet ringlets, and her face was still dripping wet. But her eyes were bright, moist, delectable. He sighed inwardly, trying to quieten the rapid beating of his heart.

'I must lock up,' he said, looking away for a second, his mind racing. He didn't want to apologize to her—again—for kissing her, because he wasn't sorry. He had wanted to feel his mouth close over hers, to feel her respond to him—as she had done, so readily. Why should he—why should either of them—be sorry about that? Especially as they weren't in the school environment now; they were on holiday. Even so, hadn't he promised her that such a thing would never happen again? Well, he'd lied, he told himself.

He looked down at her, smiling darkly. 'See you in the morning, Ria,' was all he said.

Tripping swiftly up the stairs to her room, Ria went in and closed the door behind her, still hugging the towel around her. She was shivering slightly now and her teeth had begun to chatter, but she wasn't cold. She was excited. She knew that something was happening to her... She had never felt like this ever before, certainly not with Seth, who was the only man she had ever allowed to get close. Jasper Trent was something else, a whole new experience for her, and what had taken place between them just now had been breathtaking in its intensity. This time he hadn't been sorry for her... He had wanted her. And the thought sent thrills of excitement up and down her spine. She hugged the towel more closely to her. Was she dreaming? she asked herself.

She padded barefoot over to the window and looked out at the darkened garden beneath. Lifting a forefinger, she touched her tingling bottom lip for a second. That had been no dream.

CHAPTER TEN

With a small gasp of surprise, Ria saw that the hands on her little bedside clock pointed to nine-thirty! She never slept this late!

Struggling to sit up, she rested her head on her bent knees for a second, the thoughts of last night flooding her memory. Had that really happened, down there in the pool? Had she and Jasper actually kissed…again…and had his warm, unimaginably comforting embrace been a mere passing fancy to Jasper, meaning nothing?

She scrambled out of bed. This was an impossible situation, she thought, and dwelling on those few magical seconds was not going to help. Jasper Trent had brought her here because he thought she needed a break, and the fact that in another moment of unusual impetuousness he had kissed her so fully on the lips proved nothing. Ria had sensed, almost from the first time they'd met, that he was someone who enjoyed being with women, and she didn't rate herself as having a chance of competing with his usual female acquaintances, who she imagined were all sophisticated, beautiful women of the world. She would be completely out of their league, and to think that last night's little episode would be significant to him was foolish. Besides, allowing herself to dwell on these thoughts was messing up her plans. She was going away soon—far away from here, far away from Seth and that hideous time, far away from Jason Trent and the disturbing influence he seemed to be having on her. She'd already made up her mind where her future lay—away from these shores, and to less emotionally complicated situations. Falling for another man at this particular time of her life was out of the question, and she must look on her association with Highbridge Manor and its headmaster as a mirage—enchanting enough while it lasted, but totally unreal.

As she stood under the shower letting the hot water drench her head and body, Ria admitted to being very grateful for one thing. When he had shown her around the house yesterday, and indicated his own room with its king-size bed, she had wondered—very fleetingly—whether Jasper would expect her to share it with him during her stay, and the possibility had concerned her. Because she would have had no intention of agreeing—however much she might have liked to. And refusing him would have placed them both in a terribly embarrassing position, and would have spoiled everything. But she might have known that he would never take advantage of her in that way. Still, she mused, as she smoothed the expensive bath oils gently into her skin, maybe the other women he invited here would be happy enough to conform, would not consider it unusual to enjoy a casual night of passion with their seductive host. Well, she would have been the exception, Ria thought, reaching for the bath towel.

Presently, she went down the narrow staircase and into the kitchen. It didn't take her many seconds to realize that she was entirely alone in the house, and on the table, next to a place laid for one, was a note from Jasper. It read:

7 a.m. Morning, Ria. I hope you slept well. Sorry I've had to go over to the factory, but I shan't be too long. Help

*yourself to breakfast—or to anything else you fancy.
There's plenty of stuff in the fridge. I didn't want to
disturb you. You know my mobile number if you need it.*

Ria smiled a little contented smile. She was being given
time to put her thoughts back into perspective without him
being around. So, by the time they came face to face again,
she could appear completely detached…as if what had happened hadn't happened. And that was how she *was* going to
look at it, she told herself. Good heavens, the man hadn't
dragged her into his bed kicking and screaming! A watery kiss
was no big deal! Was it?

On the long wooden table was a brown loaf and some
butter, cereals and a bowl of fresh fruit which, with a good
cup of coffee, would be absolutely perfect to start her little
holiday at Lavender Cottage, Ria thought, as she went across
to the sink to fill the kettle.

As he drove the fifteen miles to his factory and office, Jasper
had never felt more annoyed with himself. What on earth had
come over him last night, he thought, drawing Ria to him and
kissing her so intimately? She must think that he'd had an
ulterior motive in bringing her here—which couldn't be further from the truth. And, anyway, it would never have happened if his other guests had been there as well.

Reducing speed for a second before revving up to overtake
a car in front, his mouth lifted slightly at one corner as he remembered Ria's reaction. She hadn't exactly pulled away, he
remembered again briefly. In fact, it was the warmth of her
immediate response that had encouraged him to go on kissing
her like that. But…maybe she'd felt *obliged* to let him do it—
and that thought made him cringe. He bit his lip. She hadn't
asked to come to Somerset with him; she was his guest at this

remote spot and it would have been difficult for her to object. All in all, he wished that he could turn the clock back, that he had never allowed himself to get carried away. But still…it had been one of the most delicious moments of his life!

After she'd finished her breakfast, Ria wandered back upstairs to fetch her book. The morning was calm and very warm and to stretch out on one of the sun-loungers by the pool was an appealing prospect. She hoped Jasper wouldn't come back too soon…she was going to enjoy being here, alone, in this glorious place.

She'd definitely been given the best bedroom in the house, Ria thought, as she rearranged her pillows and straightened the duvet neatly. It was so prettily furnished and decorated in pastel shades of mauve and pink—and a complete contrast to the other bedrooms, which were distinctly male-oriented, she'd observed, as she'd seen them so briefly. She looked around her again. This…boudoir…was clearly the one intended for Jasper's female visitors—and only a few paces away from his own room, if the need arose…

Presently, Ria thought she'd have a look around the garden, which, she saw as she opened the small wicker gate leading from the patio, was absolutely massive, an intoxicating sea of coloured plants and grasses meeting her gaze. She stopped for a moment, breathing in the variety of perfumes that seemed to hang in the sultry morning air.

Ria shaded her eyes for a second as she looked upwards towards the series of undulating banks which gave the area a natural dimension—as if a primordial eruption had fashioned it with deliberate care. As she began treading carefully upwards along the narrow path running amongst all the foliage, a man's voice interrupted her odyssey through this mini paradise.

'Good morning,' he said. He was wearing dungarees and a large grubby sunhat, his tanned face creasing into a friendly grin as he came towards her. 'I'm Dave—Debra's husband.'

'Hello,' Ria said quickly. 'I'm Ria.'

'Yes, my wife said I might see you.'

Ria waved her arm around the garden and looked up at him. 'I am overwhelmed by all this,' she said simply. 'It's so…so…different. Interesting, as well as beautiful.' She paused. 'Is it all your own work?'

The man shook his head. 'Not exactly,' he said, 'though I am the main chap in charge. I'm up here most days, but if I'm not so well Jasper hires someone else to help out now and again.' He paused. 'He never puts any pressure on me, but then, he knows he can trust me to look after everything, especially when he's not around.'

Dave tilted his hat back and wiped some perspiration from his brow, his own gaze taking in the scene around them. 'Of course, Jasper was the brains behind all the reconstruction of the plot—and it was a tough call, I can tell you. It was just a flat bit of land when he came here, but he changed all that. Got hold of a mini-digger and sculpted all the levels, stripped off the topsoil himself. Worked like a beaver at it.' Dave adjusted his hat and turned to go. 'Of course, he's been away a lot lately but he'll be back permanently soon.'

Ria couldn't help being surprised at what she'd just been told. Jasper Trent was a man of so many parts, she thought, all of them carried out to perfection. He'd obviously had a vision for this land and had wanted to do it himself. And it was also obvious that he was held in very high esteem by Dave and Debra. Mr Perfect, Ria thought wryly.

'I'd better get myself some tools and do some work,' Dave said cheerfully. 'The weeds enjoy being here, as well as everything else that grows.'

He ambled away towards a small garden shed and, on an impulse, Ria decided to wait for a moment before going to the pool. She'd spotted the rustic seat next to a long bank of miniature lavender bushes and, sitting down, she put her head back, closing her eyes and letting the heavy perfume of the plants fill her nostrils. Would there be anywhere in the whole world—where she might eventually end up—to compare with this? she asked herself. Well, probably not…but there would be other things to excite and delight her. Being here was a temporary experience and would soon fade from her consciousness when it all became the past.

Half opening her eyes for a second, something on the ground, glinting just there in front of her, made Ria lean forward to take a closer look. She got up and, crouching down, she prised out from the earth a gold ring, laying it in her palm and examining it curiously. Taking a tissue from her trouser pocket, she rubbed the ring gently at first, then huffed at it for a moment before rubbing it more firmly until presently all the mud and dirt had gone and it had started to shine.

She sat back, staring at it in her hand. She knew immediately that it was someone's wedding band—and a heavy, expensive one, too. She frowned. Now, who had this once belonged to? she wondered. Which unfortunate woman had mislaid this precious emblem a long time ago, and may have been searching for it ever since?

Getting up, she was about to go over and show it to Dave when Jasper opened the gate to the garden and started strolling up the path towards her. He was wearing jeans and an open-neck shirt, and his black hair glistened like ebony in the sunlight. As her heart missed a beat at seeing him, without thinking what she was doing, Ria slipped the ring into her pocket.

By now, colour had flooded her cheeks. How was she supposed to greet her employer this morning? she asked herself desperately. Was she supposed to forget what had happened between them in the pool? Well, yes, actually…she'd promised herself that that was exactly what she would do. But now that they were coming face to face, her resolution was threatening to crumble…

With one hand casually in his pocket, he strolled up to stand beside her. 'Sorry I had to go,' he said, 'but I thought if I got it over with, it wouldn't interfere with too much of the day.'

Ria smiled up at him quickly. 'It doesn't matter,' she said. 'I've been well occupied.' She paused. 'Did you get the…um…problem sorted?' she asked politely—well, that was a daft question. Of course Jasper Trent would get the problem—any problem—sorted.

'Oh, yes, thanks,' he replied. 'It was nothing major, though they were right to put me in the picture.'

She was looking amazing this morning, Jasper thought helplessly. Dressed in white linen trousers and a soft honey-coloured top and with her bronze hair brushed and draped casually over one shoulder, she resembled a perfect lily, seeming to fit in naturally amongst his tall bushes and sweet-smelling tea roses. And he felt again that compulsion to inflame desire in the woman, to possess her. But there was no chance of him ever doing that now, he told himself. Last night, he'd come on too strong, too quickly; his normally perfect sense of timing had caught him out. He sighed inwardly, keeping his expression impassive, trying to hide his feelings.

When Ria spoke, her voice was cool. 'And you needn't have worried about me,' she said lightly. 'I've been relaxing, wasting time and talking to Dave. He was telling me about the garden…how you designed it and worked at it yourself.' Despite her outward composure, Ria's heart was hammering painfully in her chest. How was she going to get through the rest of this weekend?

For some unaccountable reason, she didn't mention finding the ring. She'd tell him about it later, she decided.

'I'll have a quick word with Dave,' Jasper said briefly. 'Then we'll have some lunch. Debra's left everything for us.'

Feeling almost faint with suppressed emotion, Ria went back into the cottage. She'd noticed the cold cooked chicken in the fridge earlier, and the large bowl of salad stuff. If she busied herself for a few minutes and laid out their lunch, she would find it easier to act imperturbably, she told herself.

And that was exactly what happened. When Jasper joined her in the kitchen she felt as cool as the cucumber she was slicing. She looked up at him. 'I'm making myself at home,' she said, 'like you told me to.'

He nodded briefly. 'That's what I like all my guests to do,' he said, and Ria thought, yes, that was who she was today. His guest. Not the *special* guest who had felt the full impact of his mouth on hers last night. Today, he gave no sign that he even remembered it.

'Can you sort out the salad dressing?' she asked pertly, not looking at him, and he raised his eyebrows doubtfully.

'Um…probably…if you'll give me a clue,' he said.

'You'll need oil and vinegar, garlic, if there is some,' Ria told him, 'a little salt, some black pepper, and either a dash of orange juice or a dribble or two of honey.' She did look up at him now. 'Combine it all thoroughly in a jug,' she went on in her best schoolteacher's voice, 'then taste it to see if something's missing.'

For a full ten seconds they stood facing each other silently and Ria thought they were behaving like two boxers skirting around each other in a ring—neither knowing what to say or how to act…

Then the moment had passed and she turned quickly to open the fridge. He might not know much about preparing the dressing for a salad, Ria thought, but she knew he'd have no trouble carving their chicken.

As they sat there enjoying the food, it seemed almost ridiculous to Ria that they could make desultory conversation like this. Surely, after any dramatic event, it was the natural thing to discuss it afterwards, to take it apart, to analyse it, but it was becoming more and more obvious that Jasper had totally forgotten he'd kissed her. He was, as usual, an interesting conversationalist and, vitally, was interested in her, in her opinion on any subject they touched on. Although, once or twice when she looked across at him suddenly, she found him gazing at her with the sort of expression on those formidably handsome features that made her cheeks burn.

Presently, as they stood well apart, clearing up their dishes, he said, 'Would you like me to show you around the area? There are some very good walks within easy distance—or would you prefer to stay by the pool?' He paused. 'It's a shame Martin and Heather had to cry off,' he added, 'so you'll have to put up with just me for company, I'm afraid.'

Ria finished wiping the draining board with a cloth and glanced up at him quickly. 'I'd love a walk,' she said. 'Well, I love to just ramble, actually, hoping to discover something unexpected off the beaten track.'

Jasper went towards the door. 'Then we'll just ramble,' he said easily. 'I know exactly where to start.'

Later, as they began their walk over the uneven territory of adjacent paths and fields, Ria chided herself silently. She hadn't thought to change her sandals for the trainers she always wore on this kind of exercise, but nothing would induce her to ask Jasper if they could go back for them. At least her sandals didn't have much of a heel so it would probably be all right, she thought hopefully. As long as the ground didn't become any rougher than this.

She was very conscious of the fact that she and Jasper hadn't made physical contact once since last night, not even touching as they'd brushed past each other casually. It really was the most weird experience of her life, she thought. Then she took a deep breath. It was no use going over and over it. Enjoy this lovely ramble, she told herself firmly, put everything else out of your mind. Give yourself a break.

They strolled on slowly together in companionable silence, to Ria's relief, when Jasper said, 'If we go over this stile and down the hill we'll come to quite a fast-flowing stream. Someone's made a sort of bridge out of a tree trunk—you could sit and dangle your toes if you feel like it.'

He got himself over the stile in one casual stride, then stood on the other side waiting for Ria to follow and, as she was about to complete the manoeuvre, she caught one of the straps of her sandal on something and almost fell into Jasper's outstretched arms as he succeeded in stopping her from sprawling onto the ground. Holding her tightly to him, he pulled her upright and stared down at her feet.

'Have you hurt yourself?' he asked, his voice suddenly thick. 'Are you OK?'

Ria felt so stupid—she *should* have gone back for her trainers, she thought crossly. 'I'm fine…thanks,' she said, easing herself away from his grasp. 'The only thing that's hurt is my sandal.' And the only sensation she was experiencing was the electrifying thrill of being hugged once more by her host—even if it was only a helpful act on his part.

They continued their ramble and presently they could hear the swift running of the stream they were approaching. 'Ah, good, there's no one about,' Jasper said as they came alongside it. 'I was afraid there'd be hordes of kids splashing around. They'll all be here in the school holidays.'

They got to the water's edge and Jasper went in front to

test the viability of the makeshift bridge he'd mentioned. He looked across at Ria, holding out his hand. 'This is fine,' he said. 'Come and have a paddle.'

Leaving her sandals on the bank, Ria trod cautiously forward, letting Jasper's strong fingers grasp hers as she eased herself up beside him. And the water was wonderfully cooling as she felt it running through her bare toes. She leant her head back contentedly.

'This is…fantastic,' she said.

They were sitting very close together now, and she could feel the muscled strength of his thigh against her leg. Swallowing over a suddenly dry tongue, she looked across at him.

'You're not paddling today?' she asked. He'd not discarded his trainers, keeping his feet well clear of the water.

'Nah—after due consideration, I decided against it,' he said lightly. 'Besides, I'll look forward to full immersion back home later.'

The very mention of his swimming pool made Ria almost lose her balance. Was she going to go in again? she asked herself. With him? Could she bear to expose herself to that dangerous situation again? Then she suddenly remembered something.

'Oh, look—I forgot to show you this,' she said, hoping her voice didn't sound as funny to him as it did to her. Putting her hand in her pocket, she drew out the scrap of tissue holding the ring. 'I found it in your garden this morning…'

Without saying a word, he took it from her and held it between his finger and thumb, turning it around and staring at it. And, looking up at him, Ria saw his expression darken.

'I think it's a very valuable ring,' she said, peering at it as well now. 'And obviously of great sentimental value. I wonder whose it can be. Someone must have been heartbroken to lose it…'

A sudden guttural sound issued from Jasper's lips as he clenched his hand over the ring. 'Oh, don't waste your kind thoughts in that direction,' he said harshly. 'No tears will have been shed over this.'

Ria stared at him uncomprehendingly. 'What do you mean?' she said. 'Do you know who it belonged to, then?'

Jasper paused for a second before replying. 'Oh, yes, I know who it belonged to,' he said cynically. 'It was the ring I gave to my wife on our wedding day.'

CHAPTER ELEVEN

RIA looked away, aware that she'd not only stumbled across the ring, but also onto a part of Jasper's life that was clearly private, though she admitted to being quietly amazed that he'd been married. He'd certainly never mentioned having had a wife, and Ria had somehow always imagined him as preferring a life without that kind of commitment.

She sighed, feeling miserable for a moment. The relaxed atmosphere they'd been enjoying seemed to have suddenly deserted them and, as she glanced up, she saw that set line to his mouth and jaw that she'd seen before—and which spoke volumes. She groaned inwardly. Her weekend away—her 'restorative break'—was threatening to become an occasion full of unexpected emotional traumas. But…one of them had to say *something*, she thought. She cleared her throat.

'I didn't realize you'd been m-m-married,' she said, her voice stumbling over the words.

'It's not something worthy of discussion,' he said bluntly. 'Felicity was my wife of one hundred days—like Anne Boleyn.' His mouth twisted. 'You didn't happen to find her engagement ring as well, I suppose?' Without waiting for a reply, he went on, 'No, of course you didn't. She would have exchanged that for a deal of cash—though why she obviously misjudged the value of her wedding ring is most unlike her. It would have made her a few quid.'

Ria felt herself squirm with embarrassment. It was so unlike Jasper to talk like this—to reveal anything of his personal life.

He stared down at the ring for a few more moments, then, with a deliberate movement, he let it slip from his fingers and they both watched it fall into the gurgling water and drift slowly out of sight. And, for some reason which she couldn't explain, Ria wanted to burst into tears. It was such a sad thing to witness. And what on earth could have happened for that ring—that symbol of promise—to end up in the dirt and mud?

Observing that dramatic act of finality made Ria feel more embarrassed than ever. She didn't want to *be* here! She knew that he wasn't going to give her all the details of his past—and she didn't want to know them, either. But in those few moments the mood of the whole afternoon had changed from a comfortable sense of togetherness into cold, forbidden territory.

He turned to look at her briefly. 'Have you ever risked "tying the knot"?' he asked. 'Has there ever been a time when you *lost* all your common sense?' The question was not put in a light-hearted way, and Ria responded in kind.

'No,' she said shortly. *But I would have done,* she reminded herself bitterly. *If things had been different. If Seth had been different.* 'I've already told you,' she went on quickly, 'I intend to travel, to widen my horizons. To explore the world's delights. And the best way to do that is to go it alone, with nothing, no one to hold me back.'

Neither of them spoke for a few moments after that, both gazing down at the chuckling movement of the water beneath them, as if it could provide the answers to some of life's problems. But presently Jasper spoke, his voice flat.

'I thought I'd invite some other friends up for some supper

and a swim tonight,' he said. 'I'll ask Debra to bring up some stuff for a barbecue—and she and Dave can join us as well, if they like.'

Jasper knew, more certainly than ever, that he must keep some distance between himself and Ria Davidson—for her sake, of course, he told himself, but mostly for his own. Because he was head over heels in love with her. How had he allowed that to happen? But, luckily, fate had intervened when Ria had found the ring. It had brought him back to reality. Never again would he leave himself vulnerable to the charms of a desirable woman. Once was quite enough—and this time he was going to pull back before it was too late.

Ria turned her head slowly to look at him. Good, she thought. That was this evening taken care of, then, when she and her boss were not going to have to be alone together. There was safety in numbers—everyone knew that. Although it was obvious that he had totally forgotten that he'd kissed her in the secret shadows of the pool, she had not forgotten it. She would *never* forget it. It had been uppermost in her thoughts ever since. It was dangerous to be near him…to be touched by him, even casually. Ria swallowed. Tomorrow she'd invent a headache and stay in her room for a few hours. Then that only left Sunday to get through before they packed up on Monday morning to go back to school. And sanity. And safety.

Much later that night as Ria got ready for bed, she had to admit that the rest of the day had passed happily and she'd really enjoyed herself. Jasper's friends—a few of them his employees, and some neighbours as well—had been a lively, sociable crowd who had seemed very happy to spend the time swimming and lounging by the pool.

Jasper had been in charge of the barbecue, with some help from Dave, and the food which Debra had bought—fat pork sausages and thick-cut fillet steak—was charred to mouth-watering perfection. Looking back on the event, Ria was surprised at how quickly she'd managed to relax and not feel the only stranger in the crowd. But, as her thoughts ran on, she realized that after she had been introduced to everyone, she and Jasper had not actually spoken to each other for the entire evening. She didn't think he'd been avoiding her exactly…but he certainly hadn't paid her any special attention. She shrugged. Why should he have? Anyway, he wouldn't want to give anyone the wrong impression about why she was here for the weekend. He'd merely described her as a colleague rather than an employee—which was gracious of him, Ria thought—but everyone would have known that he was her boss. And no one could possibly have gone away with the idea that she was anyone special. She was just another one amongst his large number of female acquaintances.

Staring at herself thoughtfully in the mirror for a moment, she remembered watching him as he'd cooked their supper, how the flames had crackled and flared, lighting up his handsome features, his wide brow lightly beaded with perspiration and furrowed in concentration as he'd bent over the task. And all the time he'd chatted and bantered with his guests, with whom he was obviously very popular, Ria could tell.

But there had been one moment—not more than one second—that Jasper had stood back and looked across to catch her eye before looking away again. And she hadn't responded in any way, but had been as careful, as casual as he was, playing her own part as a polite and appreciative guest.

But she'd never been short of attention from other people, who'd seemed genuinely interested in her career—and particularly interested when she told several of them that she was going travelling in a few weeks.

'Where do you intend heading off to first?' someone had

asked her, just as Jasper had appeared at her elbow with more wine, and she'd replied quickly.

'I'm not exactly sure, yet—I'll be seeing the travel agents as soon as term finishes, and leave everything up to them.' She'd smiled, not looking at Jasper. 'I'm sure they'll know what to do with an inexperienced, footloose wanderer like me.'

'So—you're going alone?' someone asked curiously.

'Quite alone,' she'd answered, amazing herself, once more, at the thought that she would actually find the courage to do it.

And, at that point in the conversation, Jasper had cleared his throat and deliberately changed the subject, asking one of his employees how his mother was recovering from her hip operation.

The following morning, Ria woke at her normal time of six-thirty, and lay in bed for a few moments, staring up at the ceiling, and wondering what Jasper had in store for them today. Her weekend in Somerset was proving to be much more enjoyable than she'd anticipated, and she felt energized and optimistic. She certainly didn't want to lie in bed any longer, all thoughts of a fictitious headache completely forgotten.

After showering, she decided to wear her pearl-grey waist-hugging sundress with fine bootlace shoulder straps, its narrow skirt just resting on the knee, emphasizing her slim legs. And, because it was obviously going to be another warm day, she brushed her hair away from her face and neck, coiling it up on top and securing it with a flowery pin. Then, slipping her feet into her sparkly sandals, she went quietly downstairs.

She had barely reached the bottom when she could hear someone splashing in the pool—that could only be Jasper having an early dip, she thought, as she went through the conservatory and out onto the patio.

He was standing at the deepest end of the pool, his strong feet curled over the edge, his arms stretched out in front of him. He was wearing a pair of black tight-fitting swimming trunks, his tanned body and strong legs glistening in the morning sunlight, his black hair plastered to his head. Ria watched, fascinated, as his muscular frame arched up slightly before curving downwards as he went into a rapid shallow dive, totally immersing himself beneath the surface of the water until she saw him strike out effortlessly to swim to the opposite end of the pool. Then he turned and swam back to where she was standing. He gazed up at her.

She was looking divine, he thought helplessly. All he wanted to do was to grasp her—fully dressed as she was—and draw her in beside him. To feel her glide with him through the soothing water. But he knew that would be a bad idea!

'You don't fancy joining me?' he asked tentatively. 'The water is perfect today.'

She smiled down at him. 'No, not today.' She made a face. How could she say that she'd never risk being in his pool again—not alone with him, anyway—that the blissful memory of the other night was one she wanted to cherish…not disturb?

'OK—well, I've been in for a long time, anyway,' he said easily. He paused. 'I was wondering if you'd like to have a look around Bath this morning. Have you been there before?'

'Once—when we went on a school trip to the Roman Baths.' She smiled down at him. 'That was a very long time ago. And I'd love to go again,' she added.

After they'd had breakfast, they set off in Jasper's car and, as they drove along the narrow roads, he glanced across at her.

'There's lots we can see and do,' he said. 'Do you fancy a history lesson, or an architectural tour, or a lazy boat ride up the river, or just to sit and drink coffee and watch the world go by?'

Ria smiled without looking at him. 'All of it,' she said.

Why had she worried that she wasn't going to be able to face the rest of the weekend with Jasper Trent? she asked herself. Their little emotional dramas seemed to be behind them. It was obvious that he'd not given their moment of passion another thought—and it was also obvious that the wedding ring incident had gone from his mind as well. Last night, and today, he was her host, nothing more than that, and he was going to make sure that the break he'd intended for her was a restful and enjoyable change. Because soon it would be back to Highbridge Manor and all the responsibilities of bringing his school year to a successful conclusion. And to hand the job over to his brother once more.

Soon, they intercepted the Wiltshire roads which would lead them into the city and, as they went past a sign which said 'Chippenham', Jasper nodded his head briefly.

'Down there is where my factory unit operates—it's going to seem strange being back there full-time,' he added.

Ria glanced at him. 'Well, I suppose you're bound to miss the school a bit,' she ventured, and he cut in at once.

'Oh, I shall miss the place a lot,' he said. 'And it's made me realize just how hectic everything is. I always thought being in business was a hassle, a nightmare sometimes, but having the care of other people's kids is something else. It was no surprise that Carl needed a break.' He paused. 'I admire my brother for the way he's taken over the job since our father retired.'

Soon, they joined all the traffic waiting to enter Bath and Ria said, 'I know it's Saturday, but it looks as though a lot of other people have had the same idea as us—just look at the stream of cars!'

Jasper grimaced slightly. 'It doesn't matter what day of the week it is,' he said. 'It's always like this—and in every other World Heritage City, I imagine—tourists by the thousand.' He slowed down to join the queue of cars waiting for the traffic lights to turn green and indicated a large hilly area over on their right. 'That's Solsbury Hill,' he said. 'It inspired one of our famous musicians to compose that song of the same name. He still lives in the area, has a recording studio in Box—the little village we came through a few minutes ago.'

Despite the hold-ups, it wasn't long before they came to the heart of the city. Jasper knew exactly where to go and had no difficulty finding a place to leave the car in Henrietta Street.

'What a lovely park,' Ria said, looking across at the nearby stretch of green where people were walking their dogs.

'Oh, yes, there are many like that,' Jasper said. 'Bath isn't all stone buildings and tarmac.'

He brought the car to a standstill. 'We've got four hours here,' he said, 'to hit the fleshpots. Are you ready for this?'

Ria picked up her bag from the floor. 'Ready,' she said, smiling across at him.

By now, it was almost midday and getting very warm, and Ria was glad she'd decided to wear her coolest dress. As they strolled along the streets, which were crowded with countless shoppers, she admitted to feeling ridiculously proud to be with Jasper. He was casually dressed in cream trousers and a dark open-neck shirt, and his hair—obviously freshly shampooed after his swim—fell loosely over his forehead, just fashionably untidy enough to make him look like a model in a men's magazine. It was impossible not to be aware of the admiring glances he was frequently attracting from female passers-by.

Presently, they started making their way upwards and Jasper said, 'I'd better show you the famous Royal Crescent first, and I know of one or two places in the vicinity where we can have a great cup of coffee. Then we'll go back, and along Milsom Street towards all the shops.' He glanced down at her. 'I'm sure you'd like to see those as well.'

Ria took a deep breath. He was putting no pressure on her at all, she thought. He was just being nice, and thoughtful—as he might be to someone like Debra, or to any friend. And, so far today, they had not touched each other at all—not even by accident.

He glanced down at her feet. 'Are you well equipped for all this walking?' he asked mildly.

'Totally, thanks,' Ria replied. 'These sandals are brilliant.' She didn't bother to add how much they had cost her.

'Hmm,' Jasper said, thinking that they looked a very minimalist affair to him, the fine straps not doing much of a support job. But, since the effect was to expose Ria's small feet and prettily polished toenails, he wasn't complaining.

Now they were in the thick of the action, where dozens of street vendors were selling their wares, and Ria looked up at Jasper.

'It's true that I only have a very vague memory of being here,' she said, 'but I don't remember any of this. Bath seemed a very sleepy, rather dull place—to my childish eyes,' she added.

He nodded. 'Times have certainly changed,' he agreed. 'Bath is a money-pot now, like every other major city in the world.'

Just then they came to a travel agency, its windows plastered with 'Special Offers', and, automatically, Ria paused to stare up, running her eyes down the list. Where, eventually, was she going to make for? she asked herself. Where did anyone begin?

Glancing up, she saw that Jasper was watching her, a curious expression on his face. 'The world does seem a very big place,' she said ruefully.

He paused before answering. 'There is certainly a lot of it,' he said. Then, 'Do you want to go inside, ask for some details that might help you with your plans? You could take some brochures with you to browse through—I'm sure they've got just the right sort of literature for someone thinking of going solo into the unknown.'

The way he'd said that made Ria look up at him quickly.

He'd suddenly become the headmaster again, her boss, with typically sensible suggestions, and his tone of voice had been almost curt as he'd spoken.

'I'll go in and ask for you, if you like,' he added.

Ria didn't answer for a moment, feeling suddenly dispirited. He'd made it sound as if he'd be quite glad to wash his hands of her now—which was silly, she knew, because it wasn't his idea that she was going.

Her voice was cool as she replied. 'No, don't bother. It doesn't matter now. Anyway, I wouldn't want to have to carry heavy brochures around with me for the rest of the day,' she added.

Their four hours were soon slipping by as Jasper continued giving Ria a whistle-stop tour of the city as they walked, pointing out all the historical sites and their association with famous people of the past. They spent a quiet few minutes in the magnificent Abbey church, before going on into the Orange Grove and across the road towards the Parade Gardens, where they paused to gaze down at all the people below them who were relaxing in gaily striped deckchairs. As she watched some of them sitting at tables and pouring tea from silver pots, Ria glanced up at Jasper.

'Doesn't it all look *great*?' she said, as they both leaned over the wall to stare. 'It's like something out of an old-time picture book!' And, as if to prove the point, a brass band had taken up position in the bandstand, striking up popular show numbers.

'It almost makes me want to start dancing!' Ria said. 'I'm ashamed that I haven't bothered to visit somewhere like this before—virtually on my own doorstep.'

Jasper moved closer to her, resting his arm casually across her shoulder for a second.

'Look at those little devils,' he said, pointing at two tiny children who were pummelling and punching each other. 'How old can they be? Not more than two or three years of age, I should say.' He grinned suddenly. 'They remind me of how Carl and I spent much of our own childhood. Sparring, competing all the time.'

Very conscious, now, of the heat of his body against hers, of how his hand had closed over her shoulder possessively— and acutely conscious of the effect it was having on her—Ria didn't know exactly what to do about it. A simple enough act on his part had made her breathless as she felt a tremor of excitement ripple through her, making her knees threaten to give way beneath her.

And, knowing instinctively that she was briefly under his spell, Jasper slid his hand upwards to caress the curve of her neck and trace the outline of her chin with his finger. For several seconds neither of them moved, enjoying this moment of familiarity.

And Jasper Trent knew that, for him, all was lost. Through no fault of his own—well, how could he have known that the woman would ever enter his life?—she had captured him, and there wasn't a thing he could do about it. There wasn't a thing he *wanted* to do about it. Because he loved being with Ria, he loved looking at her, at her intelligent butterscotch eyes and sweet mouth…and being in her captivating presence. But there could be no happy ending, he thought, because soon she'd be out of his life for ever. He knew she had a very determined spirit and that her mind wouldn't easily be changed. He pulled away from her slightly.

'Well, since you mention it,' he said, 'there are many, many other places in this country which perhaps you should visit before embarking on the Grand Tour.'

Ria looked up at him, her eyes wide and misty.

'Why not postpone your trip?' he went on casually. 'Work for another year, save some more money. You're young—

there's all the time in the world.' He felt mean as he said this. He wasn't thinking of her—he was thinking of himself.

'But why should I do that?' Ria asked, but knowing the answer. He had already said that it would benefit the school if she stayed on. She hesitated. 'Has Carl asked you to try and persuade me to come back to Highbridge Manor next term? Surely by now you've been able to find a suitable replacement.'

Jasper looked away for a second, fixing his eyes on the scene below. It was true that he had interviewed two candidates who would probably do the job well enough, but neither of them had impressed him as Ria had done. Ria was exactly right for the position, she did the job perfectly and got on well with the boys—even the older ones, who he'd been afraid might play her up. But he wasn't thinking of the school, or of what Carl might like. This was about him—Jasper Trent. He didn't want her to go hundreds, thousands of miles away from England. Away from him. He needed to see what, if anything, fate had planned for him He needed time.

'I know that Carl would very much like you to stay on board,' he said slowly and as she looked at him again in that way which sent all his senses rocketing, he added, 'and I would like you to stay, too, Ria. I…um…I mean, I feel uneasy at the thought of you setting off by yourself. I don't feel that you're really ready for it.'

Why couldn't he just tell her the truth—that he wanted her to be as close to him as it was possible for two human beings to be? Why tiptoe around? Was it because he was afraid she'd turn him down? Or was it because, in spite of longing to make love to her—he'd thought of little else all weekend—the spectre of Felicity still loomed large? What he wanted now was some space—to prove to himself that he wasn't in danger of making another massive mistake. A mistake which might leave him even more bruised and wary.

And, pulling away from him to open her bag for a tissue, Ria deliberately chose not to look up at him, not to let those black, magnetic eyes bore their way into hers. Because she got the picture all right. Asking her to remain at the school was nothing to do with his concern for her—it was all about making sure that he left everything fine and dandy for his brother. Blood was thicker than water.

She bit her lip thoughtfully for a second. She suspected he had feelings for her, at least a little—he'd made that clear enough. But that was just a simple by-product of their association, and she didn't flatter herself that it was anything more. As soon as she stepped from these shores, he'd forget her, she knew that. A man like him—wealthy, desperately handsome and seductive—could have the pick of the bunch any time he liked.

So… Oh, no—she wasn't going to fall in with his wishes. She had made her mind up about the next step in her life— she was going to travel. To escape from the past. And to escape from the possibility of getting too close to her employer. Because hers was a past which she could never confess—especially to someone like Jasper Trent. She cringed at the thought of him ever finding out. With his high principled stance—especially where children were concerned—he would never understand.

Well, he was not going to be given the chance. In three weeks' time she'd be done with Highbridge Manor, and everyone in it.

CHAPTER TWELVE

THE following day Ria really did wake with a headache—
well, the weekend weather was almost unnaturally hot—but
she knew it wasn't only that. She was feeling unsettled and
confused, and it was all to do with Jasper Trent.

Their day in Bath had been great—and very tiring—she
thought, her mind going over and over everything. After
staying there long enough to have a wonderful dinner, they'd
wandered through the still busy streets, reluctant to bring the
day to an end. But they had both instinctively kept a discreet
distance between them—and Jasper had certainly not attempted to hold her hand, or get too close—that was, not
until a high-powered motorbike, its engine screaming, had
almost struck them as the driver ignored the red light on the
pedestrian crossing they were halfway over.

'Idiot!' Jasper had exclaimed. 'Is he colour-blind?' His
arm had gone around Ria's waist in a split second, and he'd
pulled her in to his side. And, if they had been hit, he would
have taken the full force of the impact.

When they had finally reached Lavender Cottage it had
been very late.

'I don't think I'll be going in the pool tonight,' Jasper
said briefly, and Ria had smiled.

'I don't think I've got the energy to even get up the stairs!' she'd said. As she'd turned away, she'd added, 'Thank you for a lovely day, Jasper.'

Now, dragging herself out of bed, Ria searched for her painkillers before going into the bathroom to fill a glass with water. It would be good to stay in her room for a few hours today, she thought, but first she'd have to tell Jasper that she wouldn't be joining him for breakfast.

She knew she looked pale and washed-out this morning as she stared at herself in the mirror for a moment, but she couldn't be bothered to improve her appearance for Jasper's sake—he'd have to take her as he found her.

Not even bothering to put a brush through her hair, she went barefoot down the stairs.

Jasper was sitting at the kitchen table, drinking his coffee, his feet propped up on the seat next to him. He turned his head to gaze at Ria, a slight frown creasing his brow.

'Hi—are you…are you OK, Ria?' he began, and she cut in.

'I've managed to acquire one of my annoying headaches,' she said apologetically. 'So I'll cut breakfast this morning. In fact,' she added, 'I'm going to stay in my room for an hour or two, if that's OK—I'll soon recover when my tablets kick in.'

He swung his legs down and stood up. 'Fine—you do that, Ria.' He smiled down at her, his eyes softening as he took in her appearance. 'Yesterday was great, wasn't it? Well, I enjoyed it, anyway,' he added.

'It was lovely,' Ria said. 'And it's made me determined to do a bit more investigating of the UK—there are many other places I haven't set foot in yet.'

Jasper went towards the door. 'As a matter of fact, I need to make a flying visit to the office—only for an hour or so,' he said. 'By the time you've surfaced properly, I should be back.'

Presently, lying on her bed in a half-doze, Ria's mind

churned away as usual, her thoughts tumbling in on each other like disruptive insects. Jasper had been such great company yesterday, she thought; he'd gone out of his way to make sure she enjoyed her visit to the city.

After they'd moved the car to a long-stay car park, they'd just idled the hours away, stopping now and then for a rest and a drink and, once or twice, as she'd looked across at Jasper, she'd realized—with a kind of sinking feeling—that he was weaving himself into the fabric of her life in a way which it was going to be painful to unravel. Once again, a man was taking over her existence, making himself indispensable, and that thought suddenly made Ria open her eyes quickly. Because, although she knew with absolute certainty that he liked her—a lot—how far did his feelings really go? Was he just another man who would always put his own wishes first? And the thought brought Seth straight back into Ria's mind—and straight back to reality. Some men—well, men like Seth—could be so attentive and apparently caring…until it came to showing some self-denial. Hadn't Seth been the man of her dreams? The man who would have had her undivided loyalty for the rest of their lives…if only?

And he, too, had been a successful businessman, enjoying the plentiful fruits of his labours.

Comparing the two men made Ria sit up suddenly. Was she mad? Because, somehow, Jasper had made her start to consider delaying her travels in order to fall in with his wishes—or Carl's wishes—did it matter which? What did matter was that she had begun to consider the possibility of changing her own plans to suit the scheme of a beguiling man.

Ria put a hand up to her forehead. Going over and over everything was ruining any chance of getting rid of her headache, she thought; in fact, it was getting worse by the minute. But at least being by herself for a few hours, with no distractions, was giving her the chance to put things in per-

spective. Don't get carried away again, she scolded herself.
Don't let drop-dead gorgeous Jasper Trent interfere with your
life. Don't be taken in by his charms.

She was not going to alter a thing, just to please him and
his school and his brother, Ria thought. This time, she was
putting herself, her own wishes, first.

By now, with her head pumping furiously, Ria decided that
there was no point in staying in bed any longer. Maybe a cool
shower would help, she thought, as she went into the bathroom.

An hour later, she went downstairs, almost bumping into
Debra, who had let herself in at the back door.

'Oh—Debra…hi,' Ria said, really pleased to see the kind
woman's face.

'Morning, Ria…um…I've just come up with a message
from Jasper,' she began.

'Oh—is he delayed?' Ria asked, wondering why he'd not
rung her himself.

'Well, yes, actually,' Debra said, following Ria into the conservatory. 'He rang asking me to come up and let you know
that he's at the Royal United Hospital. There's been a car
accident. He was just on his way to work, and…'

Before she could go on, Ria clutched Debra's arm.
'What…what's happened? Is he hurt—how bad is it?' The
words came out in a rush.

'Apparently, another car came out and rammed into the
side of him—that's all he said,' Debra began, and Ria cut in
again anxiously.

'Is he badly hurt? What exactly did he tell you…?'

'Well, he's being assessed at the moment, dear,' Debra
said, noticing how white Ria's face had gone. She kept her
voice calm. 'He was able to speak to me himself just for a few
moments, and he told me he's got whiplash and a head injury
of some sort…'

Ria sank down onto a chair, her hand to her mouth, and Debra went on, 'He didn't want to ring you himself in case you were still asleep—thought it would frighten you to be woken up with this kind of news. He told me you had a bad headache, dear, and were resting.' She turned away. 'Now, then, I'm going to make us a nice cup of tea. I think we can both do with one.'

Later, sitting in the taxi she'd called to take her to the hospital, Ria knew one thing for certain. The thought that Jasper might have been more badly injured—or killed, even— had sent her into a paroxysm of horror, not only because he was a vulnerable human being, but because he was the particular human being whom she'd come to care about. Whom she had fallen in love with so deeply it could feel almost like drowning. Except that it wasn't the dreaded feeling like water closing over her and taking her down into a terrible depth—it was the feeling of losing herself completely in the enveloping warmth of someone who she felt might truly love her as no one else had ever done. And, even though he would have been in an obvious state of shock—not to say pain—his concern had been for her—not wanting to ring up and disturb her. Because she had a headache. A lump formed in Ria's throat.

When she arrived at the Accident & Emergency Department at the hospital, she was told that Jasper had gone down to be X-rayed and, sitting in the waiting area, watching as other victims came and went, Ria gripped her hands together lightly. What if he'd sustained brain damage? she agonized. Even a minor bump could hide something more sinister…

Strangely enough, there was no sign of her own headache now, she realized. She looked up, her eyes mindlessly tracing the pattern of the neon lighting above, the hard ball of dread in her stomach making her feel sick. And yet, somehow, she felt detached, weightless, as if she were in some sort of horrible dream…

She closed her eyes, only half-hearing all the sounds around her, when a light touch on her arm made her start and she looked up quickly. Jasper was standing there beside her, a large sticking plaster on one side of his head and, without a moment's hesitation, Ria jumped to her feet and flung her arms around his neck, hugging him to her as if she was never going to let him go. And Jasper responded by folding her into him in a tight embrace. And for a moment they stood there, locked together as motionless as a statue.

Presently he eased himself away gingerly and looked down at her. 'Ouch,' he said solemnly. 'Bit of bruising,' he explained, pointing to his chest. Ria immediately stepped back.

'Oh—*sorry*!' she gasped. 'I didn't think!'

His eyes looked into hers darkly. 'I'm very glad you didn't,' he said, smiling.

Just then a young doctor came up to them, darting an appreciative glance in Ria's direction before handing Jasper a packet containing some medication.

'These are some strong painkillers if you need them,' the doctor said. 'Fortunately, as far as we can see from the X-rays, you've come off lightly,' he added, 'but, obviously, if you develop any symptoms which are unusual to you, see your GP straight away.' He turned to go. 'Oh, and no driving for a day or so—take it easy.'

After he'd gone, Jasper glanced down at Ria. 'I certainly won't be driving *my* car in the immediate future,' he said casually. 'So we'll have to be chauffeur driven back to school in the morning.'

In the taxi which was taking them back to Lavender Cottage, Ria was longing to know all the details, yet didn't want to put any pressure on Jasper. But he seemed relieved to tell her what had happened.

'The other car involved just shot out from a side turning

and rammed straight into me,' Jasper said. 'It was being driven by an elderly man who, it seemed, was only just getting used to his new automatic.' He paused. 'I'm afraid it'll be some time before he can go on practising because his car was very badly damaged—much more than mine—which isn't that bad.' He shook his head. 'The poor old chap didn't look in very good shape, but he was talking to the ambulance crew OK. And it was they who insisted that I should go with them as well, to be checked over. Even though I told them I didn't think it was necessary.'

'Of course it was necessary,' Ria said firmly, thinking that even invincible Jasper Trent was as vulnerable as other mortals and, as she glanced across at his handsome profile, a shiver ran right down her spine. What if something much worse had happened to him? She covered his hand with hers for a moment, and he immediately curled his fingers into her palm.

There was silence for a few moments as he was obviously reliving the events of the morning, then he said, 'I'll arrange for the local garage to pick up my car and take it away to be put right.' He turned to look at her, smiling briefly. 'This was not on the agenda for the weekend, Ria,' he said soberly. 'Sorry.'

Back in the classroom on Tuesday, Ria felt as if she'd been living in two completely different worlds. As if she'd been taking part in a play. Good things and bad things had taken place, and it had all left her mind in a kind of vortex.

But, of everything which had happened, she knew that the pivotal, unforgettable moment had been when Jasper had kissed her on that first evening in the pool. And how she had so shamelessly clung to him.

During their journey back to Highbridge Manor in the taxi, they had said very little to each other, but they'd held hands all the way—as if it was the most natural thing in the world.

It was obvious to Ria that the accident had affected Jasper more than he was going to admit and, glancing at him covertly from time to time, she knew that he was going over it in his mind.

'When that car drove straight into the side of me, you wouldn't believe the noise,' he'd said. 'It was like an explosion.' He'd looked across at her. 'I hope I'm never involved in anything really serious,' he'd added.

And, as they'd gone their separate ways on Monday afternoon, he'd said, looking down at her seriously, 'I'll need to know soon, Ria, if you've given any consideration to renewing your contract with us here—whether you've thought it over.'

And Ria had merely nodded in reply, before going into her room and closing the door. And thinking, *Can I bear to go right away—right away from you? But dare I risk staying...?*

On the first morning after the break, Ria met Helen coming swiftly towards her along the corridor.

'Helen! Hi—did you have a good time in Wales?'

Helen paused briefly, nodding her head and looking pensive for a second. 'It was...it was the best time I've had for ages,' she said. 'Well, for my entire life, actually,' she added. 'It was in the most beautiful spot...unspoiled and isolated... We went on long, long walks, just chatting, about nothing, about everything...and we ate in little pubs all the time.' She paused. 'It was so good to get right away—from school—and from home, if I'm honest. Does that make me sound dreadful?' And, without waiting for a reply, went on quickly, 'Of course, I could only go because Mum was feeling so much better—and she encouraged me to do it.'

'And quite right, too,' Ria said. 'You're so loyal to everyone and everything here—you certainly deserved the chance to escape.'

Just as she was about to hurry on, Helen turned quickly. 'Have you heard about Jasper's accident? Another car smashed into him while he was in Somerset. I don't think he was hurt much, but his car won't be available for another week or so, so he's had to hire another one for now.'

'Oh…um…yes, I know…' Ria said hesitantly, hating being evasive but deciding that there was no point in saying anything or going into details.

'Did *you* have a good time?' was Helen's parting call as she hurried away.

Ria called back, 'Brilliant, thanks,' but she knew that Helen was too far away to hear what she'd said.

The following few days in the classroom passed uneventfully, for which Ria was extremely grateful. Since their return, she had seen very little of Jasper, who she knew was in the thick of bringing the school year to a close.

On Saturday morning, Ria decided to drive to Salisbury to buy some farewell gifts. She wanted to get something for Claudia, and for Helen, too—who had turned out to be very friendly and cooperative on the few occasions Ria had needed some help.

As she was going into the car park, Jasper caught up with her.

'Ria,' he said, keeping his voice down. 'Sorry I haven't been around much—I've hardly left my desk since we got back.'

'And I've been extremely busy, too.' Ria smiled, walking on towards her car.

He put his arm around her and, resting his hand on her hip for a second, sent shivers right through her. 'I'd like to talk to you—are you going somewhere special?' he asked, looking down at her. He might not have been in her company much for the last few days, but she had never left his thoughts…or his dreams. In the night hours, all he had been aware of was her beautiful face…her delectable self. All his misgivings about the female sex in general were growing ever fainter…and, although he was aware that it was not going to be easy to get her to change her plans, he knew he must have this woman, whatever it took.

'I was only going to Salisbury to do some shopping,' she said. She paused, glancing up at him. 'How are you feeling, by the way? You haven't had any unpleasant complications…any headaches after the accident?' she asked, thinking how devastating he was looking, with certainly no outward sign of any physical damage.

'No—nothing, fortunately,' he replied. 'Though I must admit—and it's surprised me—I've had one or two flashbacks. But I believe that's normal,' he added.

'And your car?'

'I shan't have it back until the end of term,' he said. 'So I've hired one for the interim.' He caught hold of her arm lightly. 'Let me drive you to Salisbury, Ria. I want to talk.'

Ria sighed inwardly. There was no reason for her to refuse his offer—and perhaps he did need to talk about the weekend, about the accident, and she was the only one who'd been around him at the time, who would understand.

He opened the passenger door for her to get in and presently they were driving along the road towards Salisbury— at a rather sedate speed, Ria noticed. She had also noticed that her heart-rate had notched up, as usual…sitting so close to Jasper Trent again, glancing at the handsome profile as he concentrated on the road ahead. And aware of his strong hands on the steering wheel, seeing the way the muscles of his thighs flexed as he manipulated the controls, made her cheeks hot. The few days they'd been apart, when she hadn't had to look at him—or be touched by him in any way—had steadied her. Well, she'd thought so. But it took only a few seconds of being in close proximity to him to make her realize that nothing had changed. She was still in his clutches…

Looking out of the side window for a moment, she said, 'I've been speaking to Josh.'

Jasper turned to look at her briefly. 'Oh, yes?'

'He seems on fine form—a lot happier than at the beginning of term.'

Jasper nodded thoughtfully. 'I've been keeping a close eye on him all the term and he's doing very well at everything— he's going to be OK.'

Ria's tongue went dry as she listened to what Jasper was saying. There was no doubt he really cared about his students. And where would she, Ria Davidson, come in his estimation? she asked herself. Pretty far down the scale, that was for sure. Well, if he ever did find out about her past, she knew she wouldn't be able to bear it, bear the look in those devilishly seductive eyes…because it would be a look of pure condemnation.

CHAPTER THIRTEEN

As THEY drove along Ria said lightly, without looking at Jasper, 'Well, what is it that you need to talk about?'

'Several things,' he said, realizing that he'd better choose his words carefully. He decided to keep it casual. 'Firstly—have you been told about the staff dinner—has Helen mentioned it?'

Ria frowned. 'No,' she said flatly. 'What's it all about?'

'It's an annual event, held on the final Saturday night before school closes for the summer. So that'll be two weeks tonight,' he said. 'It's for the staff and their husbands, wives, partners—to say a big thank you for all their hard work and loyalty.' He glanced across at her. 'It was something my grandfather started a long time ago, obviously, and it's been a tradition ever since.'

'Where does it take place?' Ria asked.

'Well, I've made arrangements at a very nice hotel in a quiet spot on the coast—about twenty miles or so away. I'm hiring two or three minibuses, so that those who want to can have a few drinks.' He paused. He turned to glance at her. 'I can promise that it'll be a good evening, despite the fact that there have to be one or two speeches. I hope you're free,' he added, as he accelerated to overtake the car in front. 'I mean, I hope you can arrange to be there.'

Ria waited before replying. 'Oh…I expect I can,' she said.

'Good—just let Helen know you'll be coming. She's the one in charge of numbers, of place settings and stuff. I leave all that to her.'

There was silence for a few moments, then Jasper said, 'It's going to feel strange—for both of us, I imagine. Carl coming back and me going—for good. Life is all about beginnings and endings, isn't it?'

'Carl will be at the dinner, will he?' Ria asked.

'Oh, yes, of course. It'll be like an official handover,' Jasper replied. 'I'll be handing him back all his keys.'

There was another short silence, during which Ria wondered why he'd wanted to drive her to Salisbury today, why he'd put her in a position where it was difficult to refuse his offer of a lift. She was soon to find out.

'By the way, Helen will also need to know something else,' he said, as if he'd only just remembered it. 'Have you come to any decision about giving us another year—or are you still determined to leave us and spread your wings?'

So this was what he'd really wanted to talk about, Ria thought, hiding a half-smile. But she'd have to give him an answer.

'I have thought a great deal about it,' she said. 'And it's very kind of you—and very gratifying that you've asked me to stay on.' She paused. 'I've enjoyed every single minute of being at the school—*am* enjoying it,' she added. 'But my plans have not changed. I shall not be renewing my contract, and I do intend to go travelling.'

Hearing herself actually saying those words made Ria feel odd…as if she was talking about somebody else. But she'd said them and she was going to stand by them. At last she had actually made up her mind. She could not risk becoming ever more involved with Jasper Trent, could not risk letting her feelings for him carry her away. She was already in far deeper than she'd ever thought possible, and there could be no happy ending…not for her…not with him. The wisest, the safest thing was to put distance between them. A flame without oxygen would soon die, everyone knew that. And, even if he was going to be returning to Somerset, he would still be unbearably close if she agreed to stay on at the school. No, her mind was made up and she knew it was for the best.

There was such a long silence after she'd spoken, Ria wondered if he'd ever reply. Then, 'Don't go. I don't want you to go,' he said. The words were calmly spoken, with a trace of menace in them, Ria thought fleetingly.

'Oh, I realize that,' she said, equally calmly. 'I realize that you don't want me to go.'

'No, because I do not believe that you've really thought this whole thing through,' he said, his voice expressionless. 'In my view, you are not prepared.'

That bit stung. How did *he* know whether she was prepared or not? He'd made it sound as if she was a lazy child who'd not done her homework!

'Oh, *please*. Don't hide behind the real reason for your concern, Jasper,' she said. 'This is all about Carl, isn't it? You've already told me that he's asked you to try and persuade me to stay on—and it would please you if I did. Less complicated for the school than having to trawl around for a replacement for my job. More convenient all round.' Ria shook her head, irritated. This was just one more example of emotional blackmail, she thought. But, glancing quickly at his divinely handsome face, she softened her voice for a moment. 'You're sure to find a replacement soon, Jasper,' she said, 'and no one's indispensable—you should know that.'

For a moment or two nothing more was said, and Jasper knew it would be unwise to press Ria any further. As he glanced at her covertly he saw the purposeful set of her chin which he'd noticed once or twice before—her mind seemed to be well and truly made up. She was going travelling and that was that.

He cleared his throat. 'Well, anyway, will you promise me…will you allow me to help you make your plans?' he said. 'I'd be only too happy to come with you to the travel agents and help you sort it all out.'

The fact was, Jasper didn't like the thought of her going it alone. Despite her apparent self-assurance, she sometimes displayed a naivety that was not only appealing to him but which made him automatically feel protective of her. If something went wrong while she was hundreds—perhaps thousands—of miles away from home… If she happened to meet up with the wrong sort of people and came to some harm he'd never forgive himself that he hadn't done more about it. And if she'd agree to let him help her, he thought, it would at least give him some more time with her…to try and unravel their relationship. Because they did have a relationship, he told himself. Surely neither of them could deny that, even though, amazingly, their time together at Lavender Cottage had seemed to slip very quickly into the background. As if it hadn't happened.

Thankful that he had apparently accepted, once and for all, that she was not going to remain at Highbridge Manor, Ria smiled at him quickly. 'Of course—that would be great,' she said. 'Perhaps we could pick up some brochures in Salisbury and then you could help me interpret all the jargon.'

Later, after Ria had done her shopping and they'd had coffee, they made their way back to the car. Opening the boot, Jasper threw in the large carrier bag containing all the travel information, then handed Ria into the passenger seat.

'That little lot will take us a few hours to get through,' he said, clipping in his safety belt. 'What are you going to do— open a page and stick a pin in to get started?'

'No, I'm going to let you give me one or two clues—but I shall give you some hint as to the places I've always thought sounded wonderful.'

His plan was going to work, Jasper thought. This wasn't something you could rush… It would mean hours of poring over all the possibilities.

'How about this evening?' he asked innocently. 'I've got an hour or two to spare.'

'Oh, thanks, but Hannah's driving over to see me tonight,' she said. 'She's heard me talk quite a lot about Highbridge Manor and wants to see my little flat.' She smiled. 'I've promised to make her a small dinner, so I must go to the farm shop this afternoon to get supplies.'

Jasper deliberately found a longer way back to the school, rather than taking the normal route, and their conversation switched from one thing to the other as the journey progressed. And, glancing across at him, Ria knew that she would never, ever meet another man who she would like as she liked Jasper…want to be with…and desire…so fully, so completely. He was, to her mind, absolutely everything. Yet he could never be everything to her. A lump of sadness formed in her throat.

And, sensing that this was a moment when she could satisfy her longing, her need to know more about his life, she said quietly, 'Why did your wife's wedding ring end up in the garden, Jasper?'

He paused before answering. Then, 'Because she threw it there,' he said flatly. 'After I told her that our "relationship" had run its natural course and that it was all over between us. Our marriage had been very short.'

There was a long silence after that, and it was obvious to Ria that whatever had happened between Jasper and his wife still hurt. Maybe she should not have broached the subject after all, she thought—it was none of her business.

But, after a few moments, he went on, 'I dislike having to admit this, but I was completely taken in by Felicity—not only by her beauty, but by her brain and what I thought was her astute business acumen. I admired the package, so to speak. She owned and ran an agency in Bath, hiring out designer gowns. She would travel the world—mainly North America—searching out unusual, extravagant garments to satisfy the ladies of the city.' He paused briefly. 'What she very skilfully kept from me was that she'd been running into financial difficulties for some time. The enterprise which had taken off so well began to hit the buffers, and she was about to lose everything. Of course, I knew nothing of this at the time, nor that she was expecting me to finance her for the foreseeable future.' He shook his head. 'Her biggest mistake was in keeping this from me until after our wedding—not that her business was failing, but that she had lied about her wealth, her situation. A falsehood of that magnitude was hardly a sound building block for a successful marriage, and if there's one thing that I can't tolerate it's a liar. When she confessed everything—it was on the first night of our honeymoon, actually—I hardly knew what to say to her.'

He waited several seconds before going on. 'But, if I found that piece of news staggering, worse was to come,' he said. 'I was informed that she believed totally in free love—with no restrictions. That a physical relationship with just one partner was unrealistic and was bound to fail, and that we should both feel free to have affairs with no guilt attached.' He shifted angrily in his seat at the memory. 'Well, our opinions on that subject were so divided I knew that I'd made the biggest mistake of my life.'

Ria herself was completely lost for words as she listened to what Jasper was saying as he unburdened his soul, and she felt somehow privileged at being told what he had gone through.

In a few moments, Jasper turned the car abruptly to take a

side road which led up a hill, and presently to an open space overlooking a beauty spot.

'I thought you might appreciate this view,' he said casually. 'And there's no particular hurry for us to get back, is there?'

'No, I suppose not,' Ria replied, not looking at him—and she did appreciate the view, which was a typically rural and peaceful part of the Hampshire countryside.

Jasper sat back in his seat, leaning his elbow on the door and shading his eyes from the sun. Then he turned his gaze directly to look at Ria.

'Now that you know about my somewhat tricky emotional past,' he said, 'am I allowed to ask the favour of knowing something of yours, Ria?'

At his unexpected request, the usual pink flush flew to Ria's cheeks and she swallowed nervously. Just because he'd confessed all to her, didn't mean that she had to follow suit. What was the point, anyway? she thought. There was absolutely no need for him to know about all her past heartaches and disappointments. She and Jasper were going to be ships that passed in the night, in any case. Why complicate matters by saying too much? Or saying anything at all?

But Jasper wanted an answer to his question. 'It's just that I cannot believe that you seem to have avoided the clutches of the male sex in general,' he said. 'That no one has captured you and whisked you off to have you all to himself somewhere.' He smiled briefly, and now she did look at him. 'You must have a remarkable defence system,' he added.

'Of course I have a…past… Doesn't everyone?' Ria said slowly. She waited for a second before going on. 'But I have only had one serious relationship which…which just didn't work out in the end…before either of us was totally committed, thankfully,' she said. 'So no harm done,' she added, her voice choking over the words.

And that was all she was going to tell him, she thought. It was enough.

Jasper shrugged inwardly, curious to know what had gone wrong in Ria's life, but knowing from the expression on her beautiful features that he was not going to learn more—not this time, anyway, he thought.

Suddenly, breaking the atmosphere which was undeniably taut with emotion, Ria's mobile rang and she reached down to get it from her bag.

'Dad?' she said, then frowned as she listened to what her father was saying and Jasper could tell from her face that something was very wrong. Then, 'Oh, Dad... *No*... I don't believe it... I'm so sorry...' A long pause, and Jasper saw Ria's knuckles tighten as she held the phone. Then, 'Of course. I'll come now, this afternoon.'

She ended the call and looked at Jasper for a second before speaking. 'It's the baby,' she said slowly, shaking her head in disbelief. 'Diana has lost the baby...and I must go to London, now.'

Jasper immediately started the engine. 'Right—what do you want to do first? Go to school—or go straight back to Salisbury?' He backed the car out and began driving rapidly down the hill. 'I know there's a regular train service to London—are you suitably equipped to go now?'

'Yes, yes—of course—there's no need for me to return to school... Oh, dear, poor Diana...poor Dad...' Ria whispered.

'You'd better ring your friend, Hannah, and let her know you won't be seeing her today, after all, hadn't you?' Jasper said, his mind working out all the practicalities as usual. He glanced across as Ria began dialling Hannah's number. 'While you freshen up, I'll get your train ticket,' he went on, 'and you'll ring me and let me know when you're coming back—today, or tomorrow—whatever time it is,' he instructed. 'I'll be there to meet you.'

CHAPTER FOURTEEN

SITTING beside her father in the small ward at the private hospital, Ria felt such a mix of emotions that she wanted to crawl under the bed and hide.

Seeing Diana lying there helpless, with her hair brushed out loose on the huge white pillows and her face so pale and forlorn, was filling Ria with such intense feelings of compassion she could hardly speak.

Her father broke the silence. 'They've told us that this was…was just one of those things,' he said quietly as he smoothed his wife's hand gently. 'And that there's every reason to hope that there will be another baby. Diana is still young…and healthy…'

A stifled sob from the bed made Ria get up and put her arms around Diana. 'You *will* have another baby, Diana,' she said quietly. 'I just know you will. Losing a baby at this stage of a pregnancy is very common—so I believe—' she added quickly. '*Please* don't be too depressed, Diana… This time next year it'll be a different story, you'll see.'

As she felt Diana clutch her around the neck in response to her sympathy, Ria felt a tide of feeling towards her stepmother that took her by surprise—and filled her with a familiar rush of guilt. Because she knew she'd been jealous—

jealous that the baby Diana had been carrying would have been loved and cared for—and wanted, unconditionally.

'I'm so pleased you could get here, Ria,' Diana said. 'And I'm so sorry about the baby—because I could tell that you were thrilled for me and Mark when we told you the news.'

Ria felt her cheeks begin to burn, ashamed at what her stepmother had just said. Because she had not been thrilled. At the time she had been green with envy.

Just then a nurse popped her head around the door. 'The doctor wants to see Mrs Davidson now,' she said. 'Do you mind going along to the lounge and making yourselves a coffee? He'll only be about twenty minutes and I'll let you know when he's through.'

The richly carpeted lounge was luxurious and welcoming, with a huge central table holding china cups and saucers and biscuits of every description. Ria went over to a side table where freshly made coffee was bubbling away quietly.

Her father sat down heavily in one of the deep armchairs and, glancing at him briefly, Ria thought that he seemed to have aged overnight. He looked tired and unhappy, and she had to swallow a huge lump in her throat at the sight of him.

She filled their cups with the steaming drinks and sat down beside him, and for a few moments they made pointless conversation as other visitors came and went. Suddenly, they were the only two people in the lounge.

Ria finished her coffee, but saw that her father had barely touched his and she put her hand lightly on his arm. 'Dad, I know this is hard for you, as well as for Diana, but cling to the hope that there will be another chance—maybe several other chances,' she said, trying to inject a note of optimism. 'I always, always wished that I had had brothers and sisters,' she said, 'and I'm certain that one day soon my wish will come true.'

To Ria's horror, she saw that her father's eyes had filled

with tears as he looked across at her and she clutched his arm more tightly. 'Don't, Dad—please don't,' she said. 'You and Diana have got everything to live for, everything to look forward to—cling to that.'

Now, he caught hold of her hand and held it to his lips. 'Yes, I know,' he said slowly, 'but I've done such a lot of thinking, Ria, and I feel I owe you an apology—well, a thousand apologies...for...well...sort of letting you down all these years.'

'*Why*, Dad?' Ria asked, wondering what was coming.

'For being a non-father, that's all,' he said quietly. 'I never gave you the time and attention—and love—that you deserved...that all children deserve...but it was hard...'

Ria waited, not trusting herself to speak. Then, 'I know, Dad,' she said. 'You were always so busy with your work, always away somewhere...'

'That was no excuse,' he said heavily. 'The hard fact is that your mother told me so often what a rubbish parent I was and...' he swallowed '...what a pathetic lover I was, a pathetic husband, a total loser—her words—that I quickly became convinced that she was right.'

He couldn't go on for a moment, and Ria hated hearing him having to explain all this to her, yet appreciating that it had to come out.

'Your mother was a...beautiful woman...as I'm sure you were aware,' he went on, 'and by nature was very flamboyant and self-assured.' He gave Ria a weary half-smile. 'And I was the complete opposite—always have been, though of course I've had to work hard at my self-belief in order to earn my living. But I was made to feel like the lowest form of insect life, and I began to believe that I'd never be of any use to you and so the best thing I could do was provide you with a good education and make sure that money would never be a problem for you.'

Ria wanted to throw her arms around her father's neck and

hug him and never let him go. How unutterably cruel her mother's words must have been—and how they would have defeated any hope of him being a loving father.

'Where did Mum go when she walked out on us?' Ria asked shakily, thinking that she wanted to know it all—know everything.

'Oh, her real love was the stage,' he said. 'That's what she wanted out of life. So she went with a group to Australia—a travelling repertory company.' He sipped from his cup of cooling coffee. 'The divorce went through uncontested and I've never heard from her since.'

'Oh, Dad,' Ria whispered, drawing him close and resting her head on his shoulder. To be belittled as a father—and as a man—must have been torture for him.

'But when I met Diana,' he said slowly, 'it was as if I was living in a different world. She filled me with such confidence that I really could be a normal, valued human being… In fact, she transformed me,' he added simply. 'And when we knew we were going to have a baby, I could hardly dare to believe that I was being given a second chance—and perhaps get it right this time.'

It took all Ria's self-control not to burst into tears. All the wasted years of not realizing her father's agony…all the years when they might have been able to understand each other and be close.

She searched in her bag for a tissue, dabbing her eyes briefly before gently wiping her father's tear-stained cheek. Although all that he'd said was an undoubted healing experience for both of them, she felt sad that it had taken the death of an unborn child to have brought it about. She looked up, offering him a weak smile.

'This time next year, Dad,' she said, 'who can tell what good things may be in store for us?'

* * *

The following week, Ria had set aside part of Thursday afternoon for the poetry lesson she'd planned. After the emotional turmoil of the weekend, she was looking forward to focusing her mind on her favourite art form, the thing which always gave her mind some peace.

She'd stayed longer at the hospital than she'd intended, catching a late train back. Her father had taken her to the station and, just as she was about to get in the carriage, he'd pulled her back towards him.

'Thank you for coming today, Ria,' he'd said. 'To support us. Diana really wanted you here.' He'd smiled. 'It was lovely to see my wife and my daughter together like that…so close,' he'd added. 'And it's all going to be different from now on. I'm going to organize things at work to free me up a bit more, so that we can all get together regularly… Life is just too short.'

With a sigh of genuine happiness, Ria was suddenly desperate to see Jasper—to tell him all about it. She knew he'd be waiting to take her back to Highbridge Manor—she'd rung to let him know what time the train was due in at Salisbury.

Now, she selected the books she was taking down to the poetry lesson and stuffed them into her bag before making her way down to Helen's room—there was something she needed to ask her.

Helen's door was ajar and the room was empty, so Ria went over to the desk and started scribbling down her message on a notepad, biting her lip as she concentrated and only half-hearing the chattering coming from the study area next door.

Suddenly she paused, stiffening as she recognized the voices of the boys who were talking to each other. They were her pupils for the next lesson and she couldn't help picking up fragments of their uninhibited conversation.

'Hey—let's see what you've chosen,' someone said. Then, '*Wicked*—that's the one I'm going to read!'

A gale of laughter followed, then someone else said, 'Do you think she's going to mind?'

'Nah,' came another voice. 'It'll be a laugh. Anyway, she's cool.'

'Yes, but won't it embarrass her?' said another.

A few seconds silence followed that while they were obviously considering this possibility, then a boy said, 'No—Miss Davidson's all right—she'll see the joke.' A pause. 'Look at the one I'm going to read,' said the voice. 'I've been practising it…keeping it real…'

'That's rotten! You can't read that one!' began someone else, before a shuffling of feet and more subdued chattering announced that the boys were leaving to go to the lesson and, as they departed, Ria stood back, her eyes narrowing. There was no doubt that something had been going on—and it was all to do with her poetry readings. But what were the little devils plotting? she wondered. And why should they think she may be embarrassed?

After a few moments, she had an idea and her expression cleared. Right then, boys, she thought, let's see if I can match your guile.

Walking quickly, she made her way along to the headmaster's room and tapped gently.

'Come.' The familiar voice clutched at her heart strings, and Ria opened the door and went inside.

'Jasper,' she said hesitantly, and he came over straight away and rested his hands on her hips, looking down into her eyes.

'Can I ask a favour?' she said.

'You are a witch, Ria Davidson,' Jasper said as, later that evening, he sat in Ria's flat and watched as she poured boiling water on to some coffee grounds. 'You knew what was going on, and exactly how to handle those little monsters.' He paused. 'What it proved, of course, is that they're all in love with you…' His voice trailed off and Ria looked across at him, suddenly shy at what he'd just said.

'Oh, I don't know about that,' she said, bringing the percolator over to the table and setting it down beside the two mugs. 'What I do know is that, by asking you to be there, they just had to take it all very seriously—one look at your face as they each began to recite was enough to stop a truck!'

Jasper grinned. 'Yes, well, I have to tell you that when Matthew—our six-foot-something giant—began with "Shall I compare thee to a summer's day? Thou art more lovely" et cetera—I nearly had to stuff my hand in my mouth to stop from laughing,' he said, obviously still amused.

'But what about Rupert's rendition of "A woman's face with nature's own hand painted"?' Ria said. 'He went absolutely bright red—nearly matching his hair!'

'Not to be outclassed by the piece that included "For still temptation follows where thou art",' Jasper said, his eyes dancing with merriment at the memory of the class.

'And they all knew that *we* knew what they were up to!' Ria said as she filled the mugs and passed one over to Jasper. 'I think Shakespeare has a lot to answer for today,' she added, 'but I'm still hopeful that one or two may have got something from the occasion—and maybe want to have another look at all those love sonnets some time.'

Jasper stared across at Ria longingly, at the sweet curve of her lips, at her large expressive eyes shining with interest and enthusiasm, and he nodded slowly. 'I think it was an inspired way to get them to remember those words they'd recited,' he said. 'They'll never forget the occasion, that's for sure. The air was thick with all that embarrassed testosterone!'

Ria poured some cream into her coffee and sipped thought-fully. 'I shall never forget it, either,' she said slowly. 'They were all so…so sweet. A lovely memory for me to take away with me.'

They sat in silence for a few moments, then, remembering why Jasper was here in her flat tonight, Ria said, 'Well, I suppose we ought to be thinking about mapping out my future…I've had a browse through some of that literature we got in Salisbury and it all looks very involved to me…'

Jasper leaned back in the chair and stared up at the ceiling for a moment. 'Let's start at the beginning, then,' he said casually. 'Looking at a map of the world, where do you want to begin—east or west?'

'Oh, I think Europe has to be the first stop,' Ria said. She paused. 'I went to Paris a long time ago—with the school—I'd love to go again and really get to know it this time. To explore.'

Jasper looked at her solemnly. To imagine Ria alone in the capital of France—or alone anywhere, for that matter, was filling him with an almost savage envy. He should be there, showing her everything, wandering with her along the banks of the magical Seine… Setting off by herself was an impossible thought.

'OK, then,' he said. 'A short flight to Paris is as good as anywhere, and then w…w…' he nearly said *we* '…you can stop off at all the major cities of continental Europe. The travel agents will obligingly carve out a route for you, arrange all the tickets and hotels.'

He didn't have his heart in this, he thought—he didn't want to help her plan her escape from him. It felt as if he were being his own executioner.

Just then, there was a short tap on the door and, raising her eyebrows, Ria went across to answer it.

'Helen! Come in,' she said enthusiastically. 'You're just in time for a coffee.'

Helen followed Ria into the tiny kitchen area—but showed no surprise at seeing Jasper sitting there. 'Oh, hi, Jasper,' she said casually. 'I've just popped along to show Ria where I've put her on the seating plan for next week's bash—she can change her mind if she doesn't like it.'

'And Jasper's here to help me formulate a plan for my great tour!' Ria said, glancing up at Helen and thinking how extra-lovely she seemed to be looking these days. Not so harassed as she sometimes did. Probably looking forward to the long holiday approaching, Ria thought.

'Are you going to join us for some coffee?' Ria asked lightly, but Helen shook her head.

'No thanks, Ria. I want to check this list out with everyone before it gets too late.' She looked at the paper in her hand. 'I've put you by Tim on one side, and Angus on the other—see? I've seen you talking to Angus now and again… Is that OK?'

'Of course it is,' Ria answered.

'Jasper and Carl will be at each end of the table—naturally enough,' Helen went on, 'and the rest of us filter in around them. I try to put people alongside those they know best.'

'You do a brilliant job, Helen, whatever it is,' Jasper said, glancing across at Ria and wishing that she'd been placed next to him, instead.

'Right then, I'm off. See you both tomorrow,' Helen said, before whisking away and shutting the door behind her.

'I'm really going to miss Helen,' Ria said slowly as she sat down again. 'In fact, there is so much I'm going to miss at Highbridge Manor I sometimes think it was a bad idea that I came here at all!'

CHAPTER FIFTEEN

THE Beachcomber Bay Hotel, chosen for the staff dinner, was classy and sophisticated—exactly the kind of place that would appeal to Jasper Trent, Ria thought, as she glanced at herself in the mirror in the well-appointed Ladies room.

Sophie, one of the modern languages tutors, smiled at Ria's reflection. 'I did hear that they were trying to twist your arm to stay on the permanent staff, Ria,' she said.

Ria smiled back. 'Yes, but I'm afraid they didn't succeed,' she said. 'It would have meant postponing my travels, and I wasn't prepared to do that.'

Even as she spoke, Ria knew that the real reason was to get away from Jasper Trent—she realized that he would not be at the school next year, but he would still be unbearably close…too close for comfort—for *her* comfort.

Sophie leaned forward to touch up her lipstick. 'Jasper's been a terrific deputy during Carl's absence,' she said, 'and I think we're all going to miss him. But Carl's lovely too—we're so lucky.' She dropped the lipstick back into her bag and paused, looking at Ria. 'Nice dress, by the way. Lovely colour.'

Although the dress code had stated smart/casual, all the women had chosen to wear long gowns, Ria had noticed as she'd glanced around her in the foyer when they'd arrived a few minutes ago. Hers was a simple fitted dress in a mesmerizing turquoise shade, its low scooped neckline revealing a tantalizing glimpse of the curve of her breasts, its shape sculpting her slim figure. Her only jewellery was a single drop pearl on a fine silver chain—her father's twenty-first birthday gift to her—and she had coiled her hair up into a chignon held in place by a clip of tiny seeded pearls. And tonight, added to her usual touch of foundation, she'd added a slick of eye-liner, a hint of smoky eye-shadow and a touch of lipstick.

Presently, everyone wandered back to join the party, which had gathered around the bar area just outside the dining room where the meal was to be served. Ria could see Helen in the far corner talking to a small group which included Tim Robbinson, and she went across at once to join them. Helen was wearing a slinky dress in a rich burgundy colour, and her hair had been cut and styled in a way which flattered her features. Ria drew her aside briefly.

'You look fabulous, Helen,' she said, and Helen smiled.

'Well, with you around there's stiff competition, Ria,' she replied. Then, 'But I have to admit that I splashed out on this.' She paused. 'Mum saw it in a newspaper magazine and was so certain that it would suit me she made me send off for it—and then insisted on paying half!'

'Well, it was money well spent,' Ria said, thinking, not for the first time, what a surprisingly attractive woman Helen was—a fact often hidden at school, where she was always dressed in a rather low-key way.

Tim Robbinson moved across to Ria. 'I can't tell you how much you've helped me out this term, Ria…lifted some of the pressure. It's been great having you on the team.'

Ria couldn't help feeling pleased at what he'd said—and it was true that she seemed to have fitted in very easily with the pattern of life at Highbridge Manor.

Just then, Jasper came over from a large group standing by the bar and stood between Ria and Helen. 'What's everyone drinking?' he said, and Tim cut in.

'I was just about to go and fetch it all,' he said. 'But I didn't hear what you wanted, Ria...'

'Oh, a dry white wine, please, Tim,' Ria said, knowing that her heart had started to pound madly as she looked up at Jasper. He was wearing a dark jacket and trousers, with a gleaming white shirt opened partly down the front emphasizing his strong tanned neck and a hint of dark hair on his chest. And the look in his eyes as he took in her own appearance made her feel suddenly embarrassed. It was the first time he'd really seen her since they all boarded the minibuses earlier—one of which he had driven himself—and his dark eyes glittered as he held her gaze.

'You look wonderful...too wonderful,' he murmured from the corner of his mouth, then, raising his voice slightly, he said, 'Helen—you look as if you've been poured into that dress!'

Helen smiled up at him, glancing quickly at Ria. 'You're almost right, Jasper,' she said. 'I had to breathe in so that I could do the zip up at the back!'

After a few moments Carl arrived at their side—the first time Ria had seen him that day. He looked suave and attractive and, darting a quick glance at the two brothers, she was struck at how relaxed and debonair they both looked.

Presently, the four of them found a small table at the side to sit and enjoy their drinks, and Carl said, 'Well, I've made the most of my time away, and enjoyed it all tremendously.' He glanced across at Jasper. 'And I'm so grateful to you, Jaz, for stepping in for me. If you hadn't been at the helm, it would have been a different story, I'm sure.' He took a drink from his glass. 'But in eight weeks' time my break away will be at an end and it'll be back to normal.' He smiled across at Helen. 'Thank heaven Helen will be there to hold my hand!'

Helen raised one eyebrow enigmatically. 'Hmm, I'll keep you on the straight and narrow, Carl. Trust me.'

Just then, someone beckoned for Ria and Helen to come over, mouthing something they couldn't make out, so they both got up, leaving the men together for a few moments.

Jasper stared into his glass thoughtfully. 'It's been my pleasure, Carl, to hold the reins,' he said. 'And it's been a revelation.' He paused, shaking his head briefly. 'And I feel I owe you an apology.'

Carl frowned. 'Whatever for?'

'Oh, for walking away all those years ago, and leaving Highbridge Manor to you. Assuming that you would be the dutiful son, I mean. Assuming that you had no other ambitions of your own. Because you were the oldest, I let that be my excuse…as if it was cut and dried.' He paused. 'But being away from the place has so obviously done you good it's made me realize just how selfish I've been.'

Carl leaned forward and put his hand on Jasper's shoulder. 'Don't be ridiculous,' he said affably. 'I can't wait to get back to the place! Yes, I've had a brilliant time, but honestly, running the school is what I'm best at…is where I feel really comfortable. And I've missed it. So stop beating yourself up. I'm sure the change has been good for both of us—but it's high time you got back to where you belong and leave me where *I* belong.'

And, glancing over at them from where she was chatting with the others, Ria saw Jasper half-stand and put his arm around his brother's shoulders, almost hugging him for a second, his white teeth gleaming as he smiled broadly at something Carl was saying. She smiled briefly. It must be wonderful to be that close to a sibling, she thought.

Now, everyone was asked to take their places in the dining room. There were about seventy people present, and it soon became a lively gathering as everyone began to relax—aided by the generous supply of wine on the table.

Ria knew that Jasper and Helen had decided the menu between them, and as the food appeared she knew it was going to be fabulous. Although Ria's appetite often deserted her on occasions like this, she found herself tucking into everything—and the main course of braised venison in a rich sauce was a special favourite of hers. Glancing up, she saw Jasper watching her.

'After this, I won't be eating for a week,' she said.

'I knew you'd like it here,' he said softly, thinking that the only thing *he* would have liked was for them to be there alone, just the two of them.

The mouth-watering desserts which arrived almost defeated Ria's appetite, but she did manage a small slice of meringue Chantilly crème, licking the last morsel from her spoon before putting it back down on the dish. Suddenly a huge rush of contentment came over her, and she realized how happy—really happy—she'd allowed herself to be over the last few months. And it didn't take much imagination to know why that was. She deliberately let her hand brush against Jasper's wrist as she reached for her glass of water and he immediately responded, pressing his fingers into her palm for a second.

Presently, he stood up, tapping the side of his glass with a spoon, and there was an immediate hush as everyone looked over at him. He cleared his throat.

'One of the strict rules of this event,' he said solemnly, 'is that no speech must last for longer than one minute. So I'll be quick.' He paused. 'I just want to thank you all for your support during my time at Highbridge Manor. I couldn't have done any of it without you. You are a really great crowd, and I shall never forget your cooperation and understanding.' He looked around at everyone, serious for a moment. 'And now,' he went on, 'I hand you all back to Carl. Thanks for trusting me, Carl,' he said, glancing over at his brother. 'I think you'll find I've left everything in reasonable order.'

He sat down to a huge round of applause and some cheering, and Carl instantly stood up to reply.

'I don't doubt that for a minute, Jasper,' he said. 'And I owe you a great debt—as I do everyone here tonight. You've kept the ship magnificently afloat during my absence and I'll always be grateful.' He looked down at Helen for a second. 'And I must add my special thanks to my secretary,' he went on. 'She's kept me in touch for the entire time I've been away, keeping me in the picture… In fact, I feel that my feet are already on the hamster's wheel.' Much laughter greeted that last remark.

'So I offer you a toast,' Carl went on, picking up his glass. 'To Highbridge Manor and its continuing success, to the tireless staff…and our terrific kids.'

Another, longer round of applause greeted that last sentiment as everyone stood to drink and, just as they were all about to sit down again, Carl spoke up.

'Oh—there is one other little thing I must mention.' He smiled around at the gathering. 'I want you all to know that my secretary has done me the great honour of agreeing to become my wife.' He looked down at Helen, who returned his gaze with moist eyes. 'I really don't think I could face the future without her,' he added quietly.

After a second's staggered silence, there was another enormous gale of applause and cheering, followed by several members of staff rushing over to give Helen a hug and to shake Carl's hand, and he looked over at Jasper, giving him a wicked grin. It was the evening's bombshell, which no one had anticipated, and Ria was amazed at the news. Jasper looked down at her.

'Carl let me in on his secret earlier, in the bar,' he said. 'And I am absolutely thrilled for him—for both of them.'

'And so am I,' Ria said, her mind working overtime. 'But that holiday Helen had in Wales—you know—I thought there was something…different…about her after that. She told me that she'd had the best time of her life, but was rather cagey about the details when I asked her about it.' Ria looked up, her eyes twinkling. 'I think she and Carl were probably there together—she was deliberately evasive when I asked her which friends she'd been with.'

Jasper nodded. 'Carl told me that that was the first occasion they'd been alone together—really alone—and he suddenly realized just how much he…well, liked Helen. I mean, they've known each other for years, obviously, but not in that way. And it didn't take him long to make up his mind and pop the question.' He smiled slowly at Ria. 'But you guessed something had been going on, while I didn't have a clue. I knew there's something special about you,' he added.

Later, with the atmosphere charged with excitement over the announcement of the evening, everyone went back into the lounge bar, where a pianist was playing some current pop music. Ria went across to Helen and gave her a hug.

'Helen,' she said softly, 'I'm so pleased for you… You and Carl deserve each other, and the school deserves you both. I know you're going to be happy.'

Helen was almost overwhelmed with happiness. 'Ria, I was longing to let you in on our secret,' she said. 'But we decided not to tell anyone at all—because we wouldn't know where to start! Jasper only knew an hour ago.' She almost clung to Ria for a second. 'And the beautiful bracelet you've given me will be amongst my most treasured possessions, Ria… You really shouldn't have done—but *thank* you!'

'I like giving people presents, especially people who've

been very kind and helpful to me,' Ria said, remembering how, on the day she'd attended her interview, she'd wondered whether the Highbridge Manor secretary would be a formidable member of the team. And nothing could have been further from the truth.

'Well, if I've been helpful, so have you!' Helen said. She paused. 'And I was so afraid that you would turn out to be rather a handful—like your predecessor,' she said. 'But I was so wrong, Ria. We're all going to miss you—a lot.'

Presently, after Jasper and Ria had spent some time in animated conversation with the happy couple, and with everyone else, he bent to whisper in her ear.

'After all that, I need some fresh air,' he said. 'Let's go for a stroll—the tide's coming in and it's a perfect evening.'

Together, they left the building and made their way down the short drive and along the road towards the sea wall. Although it was a pleasant evening, Ria reached into her bag for the flimsy wrap she always carried with her, draping it carelessly over her shoulders, and automatically Jasper took one end of it, helping her to wind it into place. She looked up at him.

'What an enchanting little cove this is,' she said appreciatively. 'Is it private to the hotel?'

'No, I don't think so,' Jasper said, 'but it's never very overpopulated with visitors—all the shingle and pebbles don't attract families with kids. And there's absolutely nothing to buy—no ice creams or burgers,' he added.

Looking down at her, he thought how exquisite she was looking—and how lucky he felt to be walking here alongside her. He bit his lip. Could he get lucky…could he convince her that his feelings for her were genuine? And could he persuade her to begin to feel the same for him?

After a few moments they came to three short steps which

would take them down on to the beach and Jasper went first, turning to hold out his hand to help Ria down. He glanced at the silver pumps she was wearing.

'It'll take us all of two minutes to walk the length of the beach,' he said, 'and, at this edge, the shingle is easy enough to manage, but are your…um…shoes…up to the job?'

Ria didn't look up at him as she slipped them from her feet.

'Probably,' she replied, 'but I'll go barefoot—I like the crunchy feeling of sand beneath my toes.'

Now he took Ria's hand in his. 'Just in case we encounter some large pebbles along the way,' he said, 'I'd better offer some support.'

Ria's spine shivered all the way down at his touch…and she knew that she was hoping he'd put his arm around her waist so that she could feel his bodily warmth. She sighed inwardly. Carl's shock announcement had made her feel uncharacteristically romantic. She looked up at him.

'I still can't get my head around Carl and Helen being engaged,' she said lightly. 'What an exciting evening this is turning out to be!'

Suddenly, Ria's toe did catch on something sharp and she stumbled. 'Ouch,' she said, hopping on one foot, and immediately Jasper caught her around the waist and lifted her up on to the low sea wall.

'Where does it hurt?' he asked.

'There—on my little toe,' Ria said and, as she bent forward to show him, he pulled her roughly forward before taking her in his arms and kissing her…slowly…deeply…and Ria responded, any inhibitions floating away on the salty breeze. After several heart-churning moments, he released his tight hold on her but still kept his arms around her waist, not letting her look away.

Despite the feelings he had aroused in her, making her

tremble with desire, Ria knew that it was the moment to bring this part of her life to a stop. Her arms had automatically gone around his neck and now she nestled her face into him, feeling his cheek rough against hers.

'Jasper,' she said softly, 'I must…we must stop this…now.'

'No,' he said firmly, 'this is only the beginning…'

'No, Jasper,' she said, pulling away. Now she felt calm, ready to put things in place. 'I'm not ready to…the time is not right…nothing's right. You don't know me; you don't know me at all.'

'Oh?' he said, loving the feel of her soft body moulding into his, the fragrance of her hair as his lips brushed the top of her head. 'Go on; tell me what isn't right.'

Ria knew that she had no future with someone like Jasper Trent—so she may as well tell him the truth. What did she have to lose?

'You're going to hate me,' she began slowly.

'Explain,' he said.

Ria took a deep breath. 'Sixteen months ago, I killed my baby,' she said quietly.

If he was surprised by her statement, he gave no hint of it. 'Carry on,' he instructed.

'Well…I'd been with Seth—the father of my child—for a year, and we'd been living together for a few months,' she said, surprised at how controlled she was feeling, how she was managing to keep her voice calm. 'Seth was a very popular man and we always seemed to be in a crowd…party-ing…having fun. A new experience for me,' she added. 'He was such fun to be with, and was always telling me how much he enjoyed my company…and I thought we'd eventually get married…and have a family…*be* a family…' She swallowed as each word was beginning to hurt. And, after a long pause, she went on. 'When I realized I was pregnant I was totally shocked—because it wasn't meant to happen… I thought I'd taken care of everything. I put off telling Seth until I was about three months, and when I did he…he just shrugged and said—no problem. Get rid of it.' Ria's lips tilted in something resembling a half-smile. 'I was so stunned at his reaction I actually fainted, and when he brought me round he was kind and conciliatory, explaining that fatherhood was something he'd never envisaged…he couldn't see why anyone should want their life interrupted, disrupted by children.'

Now Ria's eyes filled with tears and she let them fall unhindered. Jasper took his handkerchief from his top pocket and wiped her cheeks gently, not saying anything, letting her relive her distress.

'When I told him that I'd never agree to what he said, he got really angry—I'd never seen him like that before. He turned into someone entirely different, and…and it frightened me,' she added simply. 'Then…then he accused me of deliberately doing this—of trapping him into fatherhood.' She stared up into Jasper's eyes and, in the pale moonlight, she looked almost ghost-like as she spoke.

Presently, she went on. 'If I held out for what I wanted, I realized I was condemning my baby to a childhood with an absent father—much as I'd had myself. And I honestly did believe that a child does better with two parents. So—' she paused '—I took myself to the private hospital Seth had booked for me. He didn't bother to come; just gave me a blank cheque.'

Ria had to wait for several moments before she could go on, and Jasper tightened his grasp of her, his overpowering love for this vulnerable woman only just exceeding the disgust he felt for what the man had put her through. How could he—how could any man—have demanded this of her, have deserted her?

'I actually had my finger on the bell push of the door at

that hospital,' Ria went on, calm again now, 'when I knew that I was not going to go through with it. I thought—well, if my child had no father, it would have me—a mother who would always be there, and who would always give unstinting love. Perhaps one parent could be enough, after all, I told myself. Plenty of other people seem to make a success of it. So I turned and walked away...walked right away. I shall never forget the brightness of the sun that morning...'

'So then, you didn't...stop the pregnancy?' Jasper said curiously, not wanting to use the cruel word *abortion.*

'Oh, yes, I did,' Ria said flatly. She closed her eyes for a second. 'There was a coffee house on the corner of that street and I went in and sat down and ordered a cappuccino. Everyone around me was laughing and chatting—their lives so uncomplicated and normal...nobody could know what was going on in mine...and then suddenly I knew something terrible was happening to me... Then all those faces and the voices grew fainter... I could hear noises but I didn't know what they were...and, the next thing, I woke up in hospital and they told me I'd had a miscarriage.'

Ria flopped her head back against Jasper's neck in despair. 'So I was the victim and the culprit, Jasper. I was being punished for having considered—even for a moment— killing the little creature inside me who'd already started on its life journey. All the stress and anguish ended it. That *had* to have been the reason. And it was all my fault. Everything was all my fault.'

Jasper didn't say anything for a few moments, wondering how he was going to convince Ria of her total innocence in all this. Perhaps he never would, he thought. Perhaps the only thing he *could* do was to promise her the love and support and commitment that she had never known before. He drew her even closer to him, kissing her softly on her lips, her chin, her throat, and she didn't stop him because she knew it was all over between them.

'And…Seth?' He could barely choke out the man's name.

'Seth never knew what had really happened,' Ria said. 'And I didn't bother telling him—he was always terribly squeamish and wouldn't have appreciated being given all the gory details. Anyway, he arranged to be away in the States at the time I was going to be at the hospital. All he did know was that there was no baby, and that nothing had left his bank account—I told him I didn't want his money—and that I didn't want him, either. That was it. It was over between us. Everything was all over.'

Jasper looked down at her, aching with the tenderness and love he was feeling for her at this moment.

'Why did you think it necessary to tell me all this, Ria?' he asked softly. 'You didn't need to. It was your business; it could have been your secret.'

'Because I thought you deserved to know everything about me,' she said quietly. 'Everything about the woman you seem to…to want to be with.'

They stayed there, locked together for a while, then, with his lips brushing her ear, he said softly, 'I don't know what plans you have for tomorrow, but I have some—for both of us. We're going to Lavender Cottage.'

Ria unpacked the small case of belongings she'd brought, laying everything out carefully on the bed, her mind still churning. She hadn't stopped thinking about everything that had gone on last night, and had barely slept.

The staff party had gone with a swing—the best yet, everyone said—and Ria had surprised herself at how she'd managed to relax and take part in all the jollity, which hadn't ended until one a.m.

Jasper's reaction to what she'd told him had come as a surprise, too… At the very least, she would have expected him to have been judgemental. But he had not been. He had been kind and reassuring.

'I am no expert in such things,' he'd said, 'but I'm fairly certain that no amount of stress would have caused you to miscarry, Ria. That was nature's way of handling things, deciding what's best. Your baby—that baby—was just not meant to be, and that's all there is to it.'

Now, Ria took out the bikini she'd brought with her. Jasper had decided that, as the fine weather was due to end later today, they were both going to have a swim before lunch.

'Debra and Dave are away in Sussex, visiting their daughter,' he'd said, 'but she's made sure there's plenty of food in the fridge…so we'll be looking after ourselves.'

Stripping off her clothes, Ria put on her swimwear and glanced at herself in the mirror. The bikini was in a rich midnight-blue, with a fine gold edging—and was undeniably seductive. She smiled faintly. She didn't think Jasper would object.

She went through the conservatory and out on to the patio and saw him already standing on the side of the pool, his toes curling over the edge. As she came over towards him she was aware of the expression in his eyes as he looked her up and down unashamedly. His lips parted in a cool smile, then he held out his hand for her to join him and she did, positioning herself close beside him.

Then, still looking at her, he stretched his arms out in front of him, inviting her to do the same.

'Dive with me, Ria,' he said softly. 'You can do it. It'll be all right.'

Her heart rate had quickened considerably—not only at the sight of his toned, muscled body in the tight, revealing trunks, but also at the thought of having to dive head first, straight down into the water But she knew she was going to do as he'd asked.

Taking a deep breath, and half-closing her eyes, she stretched out her arms, her body poised, waiting for him to give the word.

'Now,' he said softly, and together, as one, they speared their way into the water and Ria felt the familiar rushing in her ears, the reverberations in her head. But…where was the panic…where was the horrible feeling that she was going to go down and down and never come back to the surface? It wasn't there! None of that was there!

Then it was over and they were back at the surface, and Jasper was swimming around her, his face drenched, his lips parted in a broad smile. And Ria was laughing excitedly, throwing her hair back from her face and clutching on to Jasper as if she was never going to let him go.

'I never thought I'd be able to do that!' she exclaimed breathlessly.

And, in a replay of what had happened before, he closed his lips over hers, trapping her deliciously, his overt need of her filling her heart with passion.

'That,' he said, 'was just the beginning—the beginning of our beginning.' He pulled her in to him tightly. 'There's nothing more we need to know about each other,' he said. 'Nothing to discover, nothing to put right. Every slate has been wiped clean—for both of us.' He paused, all his bodily instincts playing havoc.

'I love you, Ria,' he said softly. 'When I'm not with you, I'm obsessed with the thought of you…what you're doing, what you're thinking. And I am jealous of anyone who is closer to you than I am, until I can have you to myself.'

Ria looked up at him wonderingly. Was this all about her? And him? Or two other people in some fantastic, romantic theatrical performance?

'I've known many beautiful women—and I've taken my time, looking around,' he admitted. 'I thought I was a fair judge of character until the debacle with my ex-wife proved me wrong. But everyone is allowed one mistake, and I shan't be making another. And that is why I am asking you to consider me—in the long-term, I mean. Every time I look at you I feel a surge of hope that I can find true happiness…that I can trust the future with someone else.' He stared at her longingly. 'I am asking you to be my wife, Ria,' he said slowly.

All this was threatening to go to Ria's head. Being told by the most handsome man on earth that he wanted *her* was almost too much to take in. She swallowed nervously. 'Do…do you think that we…that I…can make it work?' she whispered. 'Do you think that I, too, can trust myself, trust the future?'

He interrupted by placing his finger along her lips gently. 'We'll give each other strength,' he said, 'and let the tide of our feelings flow freely and undisturbed. With no pressure, and no doubt.' He paused. 'And, to begin, I am going to take you to every part of the world you want to go… I'll show you everything you've heard about and longed to see. It'll be the start of the journey into the rest of our lives.'

Ria looked up at him as they trod water together gently. 'Jasper,' she said softly, happily, 'I believe that, with you, I've reached my journey's end before it's even begun!'

Smiling darkly, and taking his time, Jasper removed her bikini gently, kicking off his trunks, then letting his hands caress the smoothness of her neck, her shoulders, her aching breasts, the entirety of her nakedness, and at his tantalizing touch Ria's head dropped backwards as she lifted her face in ecstasy. Then, in the deepest water of the pool, he encased her body with his strong thighs before moving inside her tenderly. And in their intoxicating, passionate oneness, they played their part together rhythmically, no longer conscious of anything but their deep desire for each other.

And sealing, for all time, their need for each other, their trust in the future—and their undying love.

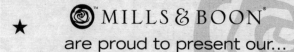

FROM PLAIN JANE HOUSEKEEPER TO WEALTHY MAN'S WIFE?

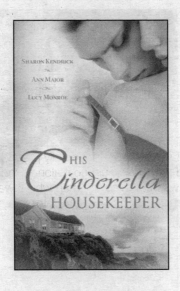

Italian Boss, Housekeeper Bride
by Sharon Kendrick

Shameless
by Ann Major

What the Rancher Wants...
by Lucy Monroe

Available 2nd July 2010

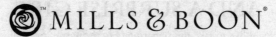

2 FREE BOOKS
AND A SURPRISE GIFT

We would like to take this opportunity to thank you for reading this Mills & Boon® book by offering you the chance to take TWO more specially selected books from the Modern™ series absolutely FREE! We're also making this offer to introduce you to the benefits of the Mills & Boon® Book Club™—

- **FREE home delivery**
- **FREE gifts and competitions**
- **FREE monthly Newsletter**
- **Exclusive Mills & Boon Book Club offers**
- **Books available before they're in the shops**

Accepting these FREE books and gift places you under no obligation to buy, you may cancel at any time, even after receiving your free books. Simply complete your details below and return the entire page to the address below. You don't even need a stamp!

YES Please send me 2 free Modern books and a surprise gift. I understand that unless you hear from me, I will receive 4 superb new books every month for just £3.19 each, postage and packing free. I am under no obligation to purchase any books and may cancel my subscription at any time. The free books and gift will be mine to keep in any case.

Ms/Mrs/Miss/Mr _____ Initials _____

Surname _____

Address _____

_____

_____ Postcode _____

E-mail _____

Send this whole page to: Mills & Boon Book Club, Free Book Offer, FREEPOST NAT 10298, Richmond, TW9 1BR

Offer valid in UK only and is not available to current Mills & Boon Book Club subscribers to this series. Overseas and Eire please write for details.. We reserve the right to refuse an application and applicants must be aged 18 years or over. Only one application per household. Terms and prices subject to change without notice. Offer expires 31st August 2010. As a result of this application, you may receive offers from Harlequin Mills & Boon and other carefully selected companies. If you would prefer not to share in this opportunity please write to The Data Manager, PO Box 676, Richmond, TW9 1WU.

Mills & Boon® is a registered trademark owned by Harlequin Mills & Boon Limited. Modern™ is being used as a trademark. The Mills & Boon® Book Club™ is being used as a trademark.